The Holiday Trou

Preface

This is my diary.

On Christmas day 2011, when I was 10 and in the final year of primary school, my parents bought me a diary. I started writing it on January 1st 2012 not really knowing what was going to come from the end of my pen or in fact what a strange few years this was going to turn out to be.

I'm not one of those people who writes loads for the sake of it, so therefore there are many blank days, which I've not included as you'd be bored, but also I've kept with the facts and more importantly how I was feeling at the time.

AUTHOR - N E SYKES

The Holiday Trousers' Diary

Right, you now need some background information to help you understand who and what I've been writing about.

- My name is Nicholas but I'm better known as Nicky/Nikki

- My diary starts in Year 6 at St John's County Primary

- My teachers are Miss Claire and Mr McEwan

- My Mum and Dad are called Liz and Des

- I have a sister who is two years older than me called Daisy

- We have a pet dog called Arthur

The Holiday Trousers' Diary

-     Emily is my closest friend, in fact my only friend

AUTHOR - N E SYKES

The Holiday Trousers' Diary

Sunday 1st January 2012

Woke up this morning at 7:30 and wandered down stairs. Nobody was up so I made my breakfast and let Arthur out for a wee. It was cold and still dark but being New Year's Day, I decided that I'd get up early from now on and do something useful. After about half an hour I heard my dad get up but don't think he was feeling well because he said something about a headache and paracetamol and he went back to bed. There must have been a bug going round because I heard my mum say the same. I went back to my room and played on my computer games.

By lunchtime we were all up and having lunch. Mum and dad were both feeling better by this time so we all took Arthur out for a walk. It was still really cold and leaves were blowing about everywhere which made Arthur run round like a mad thing. Daisy didn't smile once and just moaned about the cold and asked when were we going home?

Went to bed thoroughly bored and hoped this wasn't what this year was going to be like.

Monday 2nd January

Got up early again but wish I hadn't as all mum and dad did was moan about having to go back to work tomorrow. Don't really know why they were that worried at least they didn't have school like me and Daisy.

Tuesday 3rd January

Dad left at 7:00 and mum ran round the house with her hair in curlers barking orders at me and Daisy saying she needed to get to work "earlyish" and "would we be ok if we were dropped off at school a bit earlier than usual?"

I was left at school first at 8:15. Mum gave me a quick peck on the cheek and told me to be a good boy. The playground was windswept and empty so I stood by a wall and tried to keep out of the wind hoping someone would turn up with a football so we could run around and keep warm. I don't like football but I do like keeping warm. Inside the school I could see some of the teachers whose faces seemed to have changed from happy and smiley at Christmas to sad and grumpy now.

At 8:40 Becky and Tamara turned up so I wandered over to them. Both had had a great Christmas and were talking about all the new clothes and makeup they'd got. Somehow they didn't seem interested about my new computer games.

Eventually the bell went and we all lined up to go in. Miss Claire walked out and smiled at us all, eager to find out if we'd had a good time. She's great. Mr McEwan was with her. As far as maths goes there's nobody better in the school and he's so funny but by the look on his face I'm not sure he was that happy to see us.

Walking in the classroom there was a familiar smell of cleaning fluids and freshly washed uniforms. We were all quiet, probably a bit numb from two weeks of doing what we wanted at home to being back in class having to follow rules and regulations. The head walked in and welcomed us back saying she "hoped we'd had a good break." She then made our hearts sink by telling us what an important year it was for us as we'd be doing our SATs, working harder than we'd ever worked before and finding out which school we were going to next. Thanks, I'd been trying to forget. I'm not sure the head, Mrs Fenlon, had ever had children as she was never very nice to any of us and always talked to the staff like they were something she'd just trodden in (wish she had it would've lightened the mood).

When she left Mr McEwan asked us if Mrs Fenlon's little chat had cheered us up. "It's cheered me up now she's left," he said and smiled at us. I think he really gets it that there's lots of pressure on us.

Nothing else happened apart from Miss Claire tried explaining what the past participle was and nobody understood or really cared.

Thursday 5ᵗʰ January

School again. Why do they make us go there every day? Got rained on in the playground because they couldn't let us in early for some reason so by the time we did get in, there were 27 of us in Year 6 with flat hair stuck to the sides of our head and wet shoes. The boy's cloakroom smelt of musty wet clothes and farts. Where did the smell of cleaning fluids go so quickly? Bet the girl's cloakroom smelt of perfume and nice things.

We did maths with Mr McEwan. Don't think he was in the best of moods as some of the boys couldn't remember how to add two numbers together using the "formal method." After explaining again how to do it Billy wanted to know if pets went to school. Mr McEwan said he doubted it but he'd owned hamsters that were more intelligent than some of us in the class so therefore they probably didn't need to.

Rest of the day boring but during the evening at least dad smiled for the first time since New Year's Eve.

Friday 6th January

Highlight of the day pizza at school. It should be compulsory that pizza is served everyday but for some reason they serve things that nobody wants. Apparently schools have to serve healthy food. Why are there so many fat kids then? Surely it would be better if parents went back to school so they could understand how to feed their children properly rather than schools serving up food that mostly gets thrown away just so they can say they've done the right thing instead of making sure we're refuelled and ready for the afternoon.

Saturday 7th January

Weekend. Mum made me do my homework and offered to help. Asked her if she could explain what past participle meant and she stood to do the washing up. Don't think she knows because she said I should really be listening in class and ask the teacher if not sure.

Took Arthur for a walk with dad who seemed a bit down. He cheered up later as his team won a game in the cup. Dad's always happy if his team wins. Wish they'd win more often.

Sunday 8th January

Daisy shouted at me for leaving a wet towel on the bathroom floor. Mum shouted at Daisy for shouting at me. Me and dad took Arthur out for a walk. Dad says that sometimes it's best to leave the girls alone for a bit. When we got back they seemed friends again and Daisy apologised to me, though when mum and dad left the room she told me that if I ever leave the bathroom again like that she'd kill me. Thought about taking dog out again.

Wednesday 11th January

Snowed loads during the night. Local radio read out all the schools closed for the day which included mine but not Daisy's ha ha. Got back into bed expecting an extra lie in and plenty of peace. Mum walked in and said she was taking day off to look after me. Couldn't tell if she was pleased or not. Daisy squealed with delight outside my room and ran in saying that her best friend Kate had just text and her school was now shut. Mum smiled and suggested we make a snowman.

We were having a great time until the phone rang and mum was asked why Daisy hadn't come to school as it was still open. Daisy was in real trouble. I've never seen mum's face change colour so quickly apart from the time dad put diesel in her car instead of petrol just as they were setting off to mum's great aunt Milly, who dad can't stand.

Daisy has been grounded for a week and her phone taken away from her.

The Holiday Trousers' Diary

Monday 16th January

Snow gone and back at school. Great start to the week as we got an English and Maths SATs practice paper to do. According to Miss Claire we've got to do these so that we know what to expect when the proper tests are sat in May. Should I be worried about how well I do? Well I am. I looked round at Emily to see if she was nervous but she just twirled a lock of dark brown hair round her finger and stared at the paper. Sometimes I wish I could do the same, as she didn't look worried at all, but my hair is really short. Think I'll grow my hair.

Monday 23rd January

Have been put into small maths group with Mr McEwan. There are just six of us and only those that are good at maths. Mr McEwan says we are capable of getting at least level 5 probably level 6. More pressure.

I love maths and Mr McEwan explains it so well that I don't mind but I still feel that there is now more expectation on me. What if I go home and tell mum and dad and then don't get level 5 or 6? Is this then the end of the road for me? Will I never be able to get a job? What will future employers say when I tell them I only got level 4 in my Year 6 maths SATs? Arrggghhhh.

Wednesday 25th January

The Holiday Trousers' Diary

School residential trip. We're going to an outdoor pursuits place on the train. Miss Claire, Mr McEwan and Mrs Borrows a TA at school are taking us. Brill. A time to have some fun with the two best teachers in school and Mrs Borrows, who's a strange choice because she's rather round and won't be able to take part in any of the things we're doing. Maybe she's volunteered because of the legendary food they serve up or maybe she's there because none of the other members of staff wanted to go.

We walked into town and caught the train. It only took us 20 minutes to get there but we were all really excited apart from Steven who looked like he was about have an accident in the trouser department. When we arrived all our bags were taken to the centre by van and we walked up the hill. From the distance all we could hear were screams of delight from the other schools already there.

As we neared, the first thing we saw was the zip wire. Wow it looked mega.

First we were booked into our rooms. Everyone paired off for the bunk beds and I was left with Steven. I took the top bunk and he had the lower one, just so he could get to the toilet quicker in case the accident happened later.

We all met up in the dining hall and eagerly ate our lunchtime sandwich. I'm not sure but I think Mrs Borrows had an extra sandwich just to make sure she didn't starve during the afternoon. We were then met by our designated workers for the stay who explained all the rules and regulations before starting our first activity where we had to search for clues to solve a problem which then led on to more clues. My team won. Hooray.

We did another couple of activities which were fun before having tea. I had a huge plate of spag bol followed by jam roly-poly and custard. They were right about the food. Our teachers were sat with another group of adults who also looked like teachers (stern faces and stressed looks) and they seemed to be talking about SATs exams. What a boring existence.

After the evening activity of a "Lego" challenge and wrapping a teacher in toilet roll to look like a mummy (Mrs Borrow's team ran out of toilet roll before they got to her legs), we all went to bed. I noticed the teachers all start to smile as the Centre's staff took over for the night. I wasn't smiling as Steven started to ask if anyone else was missing home. NO, not really!

Our planned midnight feast didn't happen either as we were all so tired we fell asleep.

Thursday 26th January

Woke up really early and all I could hear was the gentle breathing of the other boys and the snoring Big Dave. Didn't take long before the others were awake and we got ready for the day's activities. Wanted a shower to start the day but none of the others did. Do I not have many friends because I'm different?

Breakfast was cereal and juice followed by a massive plate of bacon, eggs and beans before we set off for the day's tasks. Giant swing, maze and canoeing (all brilliant) before the scary crocodile creak. We were all led into a building where we had to solve clues before we could cross the creak (swimming pool). If we didn't solve the clues quickly enough they let the crocodiles into the creak and we were in danger of being eaten alive (not really). We just about managed to solve the clues in time but just as we were crossing the creak the crocodiles were let in. Screaming and panic started with us all racing to get across, that is, apart from Steven who now managed to have his accident and had to be taken away in tears by Mrs Borrows who didn't look impressed. When we all looked back at the pool "surprise surprise" there were no crocs in there. Steven's accident all in vain, but we did laugh.

By the end of the evening we were all shattered and any thoughts of a delayed midnight feast were forgotten as sleep was all we cared about.

Friday 27th January

Mrs Borrows couldn't come down for breakfast as the activities of the previous two days had made her ill. Miss Claire did, however, manage to take her up a large plate of bacon, sausage, egg, beans and hash browns though she didn't want to overdo it so cut back by not having a piece of fruit.

The last two activities were fabulous especially the zip wire. Steven had recovered from the previous day and had had his trousers washed and dried. It was as if nothing had happened. We were harnessed up and took it in turns to have a go. It's really quick once you get started. When it got to Steven's go he wasn't sure about jumping off until someone yelled there was a crocodile after him. I'm not quite sure why Mrs Borrows (who had now recovered) had to meet him at the other end and take him inside.

Leaving was hard but when we got back to school our parents were all there to greet us and give us a hug as they'd missed us. Daisy was there too and grinned at me as I hugged mum. Strange but she doesn't often smile at me.

Monday 30th January

When we got to school after the weekend we were all still buzzing with the excitement of the trip. I heard Mrs Borrows telling another teacher that she'd had a go at everything we'd done. Not sure anyone believed her.

Mrs Fenlon came to see us again and reminded us that we were nearing the most important part of our lives and not to feel under any pressure, but if we didn't do well, we'd not only be letting ourselves down but also the school. She's so nice to the children.

Friday 10th February

I love the days when we break up. Teachers are usually happy and all the children are excited about no school.

Emily asked if I'd like to meet up during the week off. We were going to the shopping Centre about 30 miles away and having lunch out. Emily's mum has just become vegetarian. Not sure what to expect to eat.

Apart from the excitement of being asked out for the day by Emily, nothing else really happened at school except two of the boys laughed at me when I told the class I was going shopping with Emily and they started calling me a girl. Didn't like this and felt quite down when walking home. Told Daisy who said I shouldn't worry and I should do exactly as I wanted and nobody should try and stop me. Thanks Daisy, sometimes I actually think you like me.

The Holiday Trousers' Diary

Wednesday 15th February

Mum dropped me off at Emily's on her way to work. Emily and her mum were just having breakfast so I had a bowl of porridge with them. When they were ready we set off for the shopping centre. I sat in the back with Emily and we chatted about school and who was in and who wasn't. She told me not to worry about the boys laughing at me and if they did it again she'd say something to them.

When we arrived we walked into the centre. It was massive and because we'd got there quite early it was quiet. First shop we went into was a shoe shop. I looked around the boys shoes whilst Emily and her mum looked at the girls. I didn't see anything I liked so joined them on the other side of the store. Emily was trying on a pair of black lace up shoes for school which wouldn't have looked out of place in the boys section. Maybe they should just sell shoes and not tell anyone whether they're for boys or girls and just let people choose for themselves. Shoes bought we wandered around for a bit staring into shop windows and saying whether we liked those cushions/trousers/candles etc. before going for lunch. We sat at a table that was shaped like an onion next to a family sat at a long parsnip shaped table in a specially themed vegetarian restaurant where it seemed that most foods came with cheese to make up for the lack of meat. I had a vegetable burger with cheese which was really good. Emily went for the vegetable pasta with goat's cheese salad and her mum chose the carrot, sprout and paneer (Indian cheese) curry. We all ate our food and left. Later that afternoon it sounded like we were being followed by a duck until I realised Emily's mums curry was having some surprising effects on her.

The last shop we went into was a dress shop. I'd been in this shop before with my sister and hadn't really taken any notice of what the clothes were like. Emily had other plans and chose three lovely outfits that she wanted to try on. Each one she came out of the changing room and asked us what we thought. All three looked fantastic on her and in the end she chose a light blue dress with a pink bow at the back. Not sure why but I left the shop thinking it would be nice if boys had this choice when buying clothes.

The Holiday Trousers' Diary

Monday 20th February

Back to school and the usual visit from Mrs Fenlon reminding us about the importance of SATs. Why does she do this? I'm already nervous about taking them and I think others are as well. Miss Claire waited for Mrs Fenlon to leave and then lifted the mood by asking us what we'd done over the half term break. The two boys who'd laughed at me had a really exciting holiday as they'd played on their computer games for a week. Their brains must be scrambled. No wonder they try to mock others it's because their lives are so dull. Anyway, we'd just got to Steven about to tell us he'd bought some new trousers when Mrs Fenlon came back in. She heard what we were talking about and beckoned Miss Claire out of the room. We couldn't tell what was being said but when

The Holiday Trousers' Diary

Miss Claire came back in I think she'd been crying and all stories relating to trousers and holidays were stopped and the talk turned to the apostrophe for contractions and ownership. YAWN.

Thursday 23rd February

Got back from school thinking about next week. Only a few days to go before we find out which secondary school we are going to. Mum says I'll probably go to the same one as Daisy which I don't mind because I like the dark blue uniform and I think that's where Emily is going too. Don't know why but I got butterflies in my stomach. Another thing to worry about.

Tuesday 28th February

Daisy has been teasing me about high school because she knows I'm worried about finding out where I'm going tomorrow. Actually I'm not scared of finding out, I'm scared of going there. She told me that all new children are pelted with wet sponges when they walk in and have to look for the blue goldfish in the toilets. Don't know what they are but when you look really closely they flush the toilet. Are all big brothers and sisters horrid or is high school as they tell us? Scared.

Thursday 1st March

Just as we were leaving school Miss Claire gave us each an envelope with our names on. Under strict instruction we couldn't open them unless with a parent. Mum picked me up and we opened it straight away. Yesss, I'm going to the same school as Daisy, Hawthorn High. Emily and her mum opened their letter too and we're both going to the same place. Hope the blue goldfish have swum away so I don't have to look for them. A little less worry but now leaving St John's seems so much nearer.

Friday 2nd March

School (well Year 6) was a buzz of excitement with everyone wanting to know if we'd got the school we wanted, most had. Mrs Fenlon joined us for register and told us the hard work starts now if we want to get into good groups for high school. She's a witch. Why can't she give us a rest? Alfie started to cry and had to be taken out the class by Mr McEwan who assured him that everything would be fine as long as he did his best and to ignore Mrs Fenlon as she just seemed to want to scare us all. To be honest she was doing a good job. The rest of the day was quite dull apart from Miss Claire sitting on a wooden table at the back of the class and it cracking down the middle. We all laughed, even Miss Claire. Mrs Fenlon heard this and scowled through the window in the door but thankfully didn't come in.

Tuesday 6th March

Sometimes I worry about Mr McEwan but he does make everyone laugh. We were doing maths when the fire alarm went off. "Don't worry" he said "They're only testing the bell." He then started to dance at the front of class and said that it was one of his favourite tunes to dance to. When all the laughing died down we went back to fractions. Am I ever going to use this apart from maybe boasting about knowing the fractions of pizza/pie/cake everyone eats?

We had pizza for tea so I happily explained to everyone how much they were eating. Daisy told me to shut up and not be so boring, so I guess I'm not going to be boasting again.

The Holiday Trousers' Diary

Saturday 10th March

Dad took me to a football match today because he thought I needed a distraction from school. I hate football but have to pretend I'm excited so I don't upset dad. There's a strange smell of burgers and pies at these places and as soon as the whistle is blown to start the game dad starts questioning everything about the referee and the ability of the players. I've just looked up the word in the dictionary he used and apparently dad was suggesting the ref didn't have parents. Strange, how did he know and why remind him? Poor fella! Anyway the game finished after what seemed like hours and we lost two nil with goals from Jammy Sod and Ugly Git. I know people have to have nicknames but these are weird.

Dad didn't talk all the way home and went straight to the pub as soon as we got back. Mum and Daisy had been shopping and seemed to have had a lovely time. They both smelt of perfume and chatted loudly whilst making some tea. I just went to my room quite jealous and played on my computer.

Monday 12th March

Assessment week at school. Again! More tests. Surely they must've run out of these but we've done so many I can't remember whether I've completed these before or not.

Emily noticed my hair getting longer and asked when I was getting it cut. Told her I'm going for a change of image. She smiled and said she thought it would suit me. Happy feeling for first time this week.

Got home and mum suggested I needed a hair-cut. How have parents got this annoying knack of knowing you're happy and then making you feel flat again? Explained that I wanted a change of image but she thought it was silly as boys didn't have long hair these days, perhaps in the 70's though. Mum has no idea. Went up to room and sat on my bed feeling glum. Told Daisy when she came in and said it was a cool idea. Happy again.

Friday 23rd March

Breaking up for Easter. We had a special assembly today where children were presented with an Easter egg and certificate if they had 100% attendance. After assembly Mr McEwan told us to keep the certificates so we could show them to prospective employers in years to come as it might be the only thing we ever manage to achieve whilst at school. I think he was joking but I've put mine safely in my sock drawer just in case.

All the staff were really happy and they were having a bit of fun and a few jokes with us. I thought it was because they were breaking up but then we found out Mrs Fenlon had pneumonia and was off ill. Wouldn't it be awful to work for someone you hated?

Just as we were leaving school Miss Claire gave us all some homework, which consisted of practice questions for our SATs and a diary writing task. "Just to keep you up to speed," she told us. When aren't we these days? When I got home mum was in the same mood as school and reminded me that SATs weren't far off. Thanks. Went to room and watched TV on my own wishing I was anywhere else.

Friday 30th March

Good Friday. Mum in really good mood as she can now stuff her face with chocolate after having given it up for Lent. Mum celebrated by having a Cadbury's crème egg with chocolate fingers as soldiers for breakfast. Hope dad takes the hint and gets her a big chocolate egg on Sunday otherwise he could be in real trouble. Think mum is mad but at the same time quite like it.

Sunday 1st April

Easter Sunday. Dad's in trouble. No chocolate egg for mum. She went ballistic. He wasn't allowed to watch the football on TV and was made to sit through a musical that mum liked and who sang all the way through with me and Daisy joining in. It was great fun especially when mum sang in a shouty voice as soon as dad fell asleep. He didn't fall asleep again and cheered up when the credits at the end started.

When it had finished I went up to my room and surfed the internet looking for local events to suggest for tomorrow to help get dad out of trouble. Didn't find anything. He's going to have to find something on his own.

The Holiday Trousers' Diary

Monday 2nd April

Boring. Dad decided we'd go to the coast to walk Arthur on the seafront. After sitting in a traffic jam for three hours we turned round and came home again. Dad was in trouble again for not checking the traffic before we left. Sometimes he can't win.

Text Emily. Her family had been to a "Fashion Through the Ages" exhibition and had had a great time. She couldn't believe what the fashionable woman had to wear in the past. Even men had starched collars for their shirts which must have been uncomfortable. Felt really fed up as others seemed to be having better time than me and mum and dad were still arguing.

AUTHOR - N E SYKES

Tuesday 10th April

Back to school and my birthday. When I got up there were six cards on the table which I opened. Inside mum and dad's there was a voucher for a haircut at the top men's salon in the town. Thanks! I'm growing my hair! They'd also bought me a SATs revision guide (why?) and new phone which was brilliant. Daisy gave me a card which said "to the best brother in the world." Think mum bought it for her.

At school nobody remembered and everyone was grumpy. Mrs Fenlon had recovered from illness and was in school frightening all the teachers again. Even Miss

The Holiday Trousers' Diary

Claire was unusually quiet. Mr McEwan told us Mrs Fenlon was back and how pleased all the staff were. By the look on his face I don't think he was being totally honest because he laughed and shook his head mouthing, "No we're not" silently.

When it was time to go home Emily handed me a card and a present saying she hadn't forgotten and that I was her best friend. I opened the present when I got home. It was a book on fashion. Apparently I seemed interested in her day out and she thought I'd like it. This made my day.

Tea was fajitas followed by jelly and ice cream. Think I'm a bit too old for that now but the fajitas were great. Mum and dad were talking properly again as mum had now forgiven him after he bought her a one pound bar of chocolate. Funny how chocolate seems to make everything right.

Wednesday 2nd May

Less than a week to SATs. Miss Claire says we are just about there but this week we'll be doing more practices. At least there's only one more week and then freedom, well sort of.

Mr McEwan made us laugh as the fire alarm went off and he started dancing again. Normally this is fine, but this time it went off because someone had burnt some toast in the kitchen and we had to evacuate the school. Weird that it happened at exactly the same time as we have our weekly test. We all had to stand in the car park but year 2 were having a superheroes day and Mrs Evans was dressed up as Wonder Woman. When the fire brigade arrived and had checked the building several of them went up to her for a chat. She seemed very popular.

Monday 7th May

Miss Claire assured us that these tests weren't as bad as we think. Mr McEwan told us that we've been fantastic and as long as we do our best nothing more can be asked of us. Mrs Fenlon said that if we don't do as well as we can then we've let the school down. Why does this one person demoralise us so much? The tests today were spelling and the short writing test. Mrs Fenlon read the spelling test out to us. She said the words so slowly she may as well have spelt them out for us. Doddle. Feel much better. Emily thought they were ok too. Steven looked worried though and fidgeted in his seat. Think he might have put on the wrong trousers.

Friday 11th May

Tests all over. We had a party in class. Shame five people missed it as they were off school with illness, probably stress according to Mr McEwan.

When I got home mum said that we were going to the seaside on Sunday and if I wanted I could bring a friend. I messaged Emily who was also excited and we spent an hour chatting by text.

The Holiday Trousers' Diary

Sunday 13th May

Mum took me, Daisy, Emily and Arthur to the seaside. Dad stayed at home because his team were live on telly in a really important game where they might finish 11th instead of 12th in the league. Wow.

Arthur had wind and we kept having to open the car windows. After an hour we pulled into the car park and let Arthur out the car. He immediately ran to the front of the car where he did his triangular dance and dropped a large deposit on the tarmac. Hopefully windows closed on the way home.

We walked down to the beach where the sea was out and there was a huge expanse of sand for Arthur to run on. He was like a dog possessed as he ran round with what looked like a smile on his face. After an hour of walking and the dog sniffing countless numbers of other dog's bums, we walked onto the promenade. We all had fish and chips out of newspaper and stared out to sea as we ate them. When finished mum suggested we go into town and have a look round the shops. The first shop was really boring and I stood outside with Arthur whilst the girls went in. Peering through the window I could see them all picking up things from the shelves and chatting excitedly about what they'd found. Looked like a shop selling tat to me but they looked happy. Next was a department store where mum looked after Arthur and I went in with Daisy and Emily. They went straight for the makeup counter. I looked on, amazed at all the different colours, slightly envious that I wasn't part of the conversation. Next came the clothes department, again I felt a pang of jealousy. I really felt like joining in with the girls about the clothes but didn't feel as I should as obviously boys don't do that sort of thing. Felt a bit down when we left the shop.

Our trip home was a lot better than the trip there as Arthur didn't produce any wind of note. We dropped off Emily and went home. Dad was at the pub so we all had a cup of tea and started staring at our phones to see what everyone else had been up to.

Tuesday 3rd July

SATs results day. Miss Claire smiled and said we'd done ok. Mr McEwan said our maths results were pretty good and we should be very proud of ourselves. Mrs Fenlon scowled at us throughout the day whenever she saw us. Mr McEwan said not to worry as we'd probably not see much of her from now on as she'd be stuck in her office trying to find excuses for why we'd not all got level 5's in everything. We'd all done our best. What's the problem?

Friday 20th July

Today we left primary school. We all cried, even the teachers. Most of us are going to the same school but a couple are moving out the area so it was a sad farewell to them. Well, not really, I didn't like them. I still said I'd miss them but secretly I couldn't care less. Emily promised to text every day, even though she was off to France for four weeks and the two weeks she wasn't we were in Spain, so we weren't going to see each other until we started our new school.

Mum was sympathetic about how I felt when I got home but when dad got back he didn't seem to care and just said that at my next school I'd become a man and it was an exciting time. Not sure I'm looking forward to either.

Sunday 12th August

Off to Spain to the "all inclusive" "Hotel Fiesta" on the Costa Del Sol.

When we got there we were welcomed with drinks and very smiley reps from the holiday company who told us which rooms we were in, where the beach was and where to get our food. They seemed overly excited to see us and not sure it was altogether genuine but I suppose that's what they get paid for. Mum and dad had their own room and I had to share with Daisy in the room adjoining theirs. Daisy had brought the biggest suitcase ever and had stuffed it full of clothes, in fact, I think she'd bought all her clothes, with the exception of her winter coat. She hung them up in the wardrobe and left me two hangers for mine, thanks. I used the two hangers and left the rest of my stuff in the suitcase as I thought if I didn't wear them at least I wouldn't have as much to pack when we left.

Dinner later was lovely as we could choose exactly what we wanted and as much as we wanted. Mum and dad had massive platefuls with numerous glasses of lager.

Think dad may be even larger when we go home. We

then went for a walk in the nearby town to the evening

market. It was brilliant. There was loads to buy and all

the people were talking in different languages. Daisy

wanted a pair of brightly coloured trousers that had

flowery patterns on. I looked at them with envy as I

fancied a pair too. I plucked up the courage and asked

mum if I could have a pair too as everyone seemed to wear

what they liked over here. Mum thought about it for a

few seconds and said yes. Result. Dad said I'd look "a bit

gay" in them. Daisy thought it was a cool idea and so I

ignored dad and let Daisy help me choose a pair. They

were a pinky red colour with a large print of a flower

down both legs. Dad walked off and started moaning at

The Holiday Trousers' Diary

mum about buying me the trousers. I smiled, wondering what they were going to look like on. I couldn't wait until we got back to the hotel.

Once back I tried them on. Daisy thought they looked cool. So did I! I felt really happy until dad saw them and he just walked off without saying a word and went down for another beer. Mum thought they looked lovely but she didn't look happy. I had mixed emotions. Excited about the trousers, sad about dad.

Monday 13th August

Woke up and decided I'd only wear the trousers in my room because I was worried mum and dad might fall out. Texted Emily and told her all about them and she said I should send her a picture. Chickened out thinking

she might laugh at me, or worse tell others and share my

picture on the internet. Wore my shorts to breakfast. Dad

looked a little bleary eyed but managed to eat a full fry

up plus toast and croissants, obviously lager makes you

hungry. Sat in the sun and swam in the pool all day.

Great to relax and forget about last night. Mum and dad

seemed ok again.

Sunday 26th August

Came back home today. All a bit down about coming

away. Mum and dad because they're going back to work

and they'll have to start thinking about cooking again,

Daisy because she's going back to school and me going

to start a new school. Reality has just caught up with me. Very frightened. And what if Daisy mentions my trousers I bought? I'll be the laughing stock of the school. Must remember to tell Emily not to say anything.

Tuesday 28th August

Went round to Emily's. First time I've seen her for nearly six weeks. She told me all about her holiday that she hadn't already in the texts we'd shared. I loved the story of her mum leaving some smelly French cheese out in the kitchen overnight and how they thought some animal had crawled in and died, so they spent an hour looking under tables, chairs even the floor before they realised.

She asked me about my purchase but I said I'd been too scared to send a photo because I thought she might laugh. Think this upset her a little as she said she'd never do that and best friends wouldn't put each other down. Realised I had the best friend I could ask for. Promised I'd show her the trousers and wear them for her so she could see.

We talked about starting school next week and realised that we both had the same fears and that part of the summer had been taken up with worrying.

Wednesday 5th September

Started new school today. Mum took me, Daisy and Emily and dropped us off at the front gate. Loads of older boys and girls stared at us as we walked through with Daisy saying hi to some of them. Me and Emily, along with 90ish others stood out like sore thumbs in our new uniform and poor sense of direction. There was a teacher standing by the entrance who was directing the new children in. He wasn't like the primary teachers for some reason. He was tall, bald, wore clothes that only just fitted and had an aggressive voice barking out directions and not really helping any of us feel any more comfortable. Found out later he was the PE teacher, Mr Eagle. Wonder if he's known as bald Eagle? More fear.

Once inside the size of the building was nothing like our last school and I was immediately overcome with the fear of never being able to find my way round. Daisy said you get used to it quite quickly but I wasn't so sure and so stuck by Emily, even though we were in different registration groups. Eventually we found our rooms and said I'd see Emily at the end of the day if I couldn't find her before. She smiled at me but I could tell she was more scared than she let on.

Didn't know many in my class only people who I wasn't friends with before but at least I knew them. Sat next to Oliver, a strange looking boy with greasy hair who smelt of chips. Don't think we'll be best friends any time soon. Did though, talk to a girl called Jess who seemed nice so I might try and sit with her tomorrow. Our form teacher is called Mrs Jones who shouted a lot probably because we were all taller than her already and also half her weight. You could easily lose her in a crowded school unless she was playing hide and seek and trying to hide behind a lamppost.

Not sure how we got to 3:00pm quite so quickly as each different class seemed to last an eternity with life now being ruled by a bell being rung every 50 minutes and then a 10 minute walk trying to find where we were supposed to be going next with other children deliberately telling us the wrong directions and thinking it was funny. Leaving school was great apart from the realisation that I'd still got another 7 years minus one day still to go. How am I going to survive? Didn't see any blue goldfish or wet sponges though.

Mum met us at the front of school but wish she hadn't as she gave me a big kiss just as two hundred year 8 and 9's walked through the gate. There were loads of jeers and shouts of mummy's boy along with giggling. Emily quickly joined us beaming from ear to ear. She'd had a good day.

Friday 7th September

Last day of the week. School hadn't got better apart from I could now find half the classrooms in under five minutes, the other half still being a bit of a mystery. My hair, which was now getting quite long, was getting a bit of attention. Most of the boys had a number one cut and they were the ones who seemed most intent on laughing or calling me names. Thought about getting it cut but decided against it, though couldn't quite put my finger on why.

Double chemistry was the highlight of the day as our teacher Mr Janson showed us some tricks with chemicals. He wasn't very good and several people on the front row got covered in an orange type slime and had to be taken to first aid after his first demonstration. Mr Janson then showed us how to light a Bunsen burner, again without much success until eventually it worked but he managed to singe his hair. The whole class laughed. I felt sorry for him as my whole life seems to be doing things but not quite right just like his.

Sunday 9th September

Went round to Emily's. We talked for ages about school. She was enjoying it but I wasn't and was finding it all a little stressful. I told her about the others laughing at my hair now being long. She assured me that it looked great and then surprised me by getting a bobble and tying it back into a pony tail. She said it looked even better and really suited me. My heart leapt and I felt a bit conscious of it but didn't take it out. Emily said I could keep it so that whenever I wanted I could tie my hair back. I love Emily, she so seems to understand me even though I don't. Left the bobble in when I went home. Mum eyed me a little suspiciously and dad laughed asking if I'd been for an audition with Status Quo (who are they?). Again feelings of happiness were extinguished quickly.

Friday 19th October

The Holiday Trousers' Diary

Breaking up for half term. School hasn't got any better and I still feel different to everyone else but don't know why. In assembly Mr Eagle told us to have a good break as we'd probably never worked as hard in our lives as we had done this term. Obviously he's never spoken to the teachers at primary school who think the same. Looking round, the fresh faced newly uniformed children of seven weeks again had now morphed into scruffy replicas of all the other children and telling the difference was now difficult apart from the fact all the year 7's were standing at the front of hall. I left school with a spring in my step. I'd managed the first half term and was still alive. Result.

Had a bath tonight. Was just about to get in when I noticed Daisy had left a dress hanging in the bathroom.

It was the exact same one Emily had bought all those months ago. Don't know why but for a laugh thought I'd try it on. I took it off the hanger and my hands were trembling. I stepped into it and put my arms through before doing the buttons up the front. It fitted perfectly. I looked in the mirror and spun around enjoying the look of the dress and the feeling of it being right. I stopped and noticed I was smiling. I took the dress off, hung it back up, got in the bath, turned the tap on and cried. This isn't right, I shouldn't feel this way. What's wrong with me?

Saturday 20th October

Slept terribly last night. Couldn't stop thinking about that dress and how it felt so right but so wrong at the same time. Mustn't do it again. I must conform.

Friday 26th October

Have spent the week doing homework and worrying about who or what I am. It's been horrible. I'm so confused. Even Daisy's noticed that something's wrong and has asked me a couple of times if I'm ok which I'm surprised about because the only thing she seems interested in at the moment is Davy Clarke in Year 10 who's captain of the football team. I know he's tall and good looking but he's also got a lazy eye. Dad says they should mention his good eye as that's the only bit of him that isn't lazy. She's been to the pictures with him a couple of times and manages to mention his name every time we talk at home, on any subject. It won't last. Anyway I assured her I was ok and said it was just the amount of work I had. She seemed to accept this but gave me a knowing look when she left my room, or am I just reading too much into it?

Monday 29th October

Back at school. Emily was off poorly today so I didn't have my usual lunch partner. I sat down with Oliver who wasn't quite as bad as I first thought. He'd managed to pick up a new nickname and was known around school as Oliver Oil because he still had greasy hair and still smelt of chips. I asked him what his favourite food was and surprisingly found out it was chips. Who'd have thought? He also told me he quite liked Emily and was wondering if I could mention it to her and see what her reaction was like. I told him I would but secretly thought I knew the answer. Also I didn't want him coming between us, not that she's my girlfriend, she's my best mate. I suppose I was a bit jealous that someone else was thinking like that.

Lunch finished we wandered onto the large field at the back of the school. We were both met by shouted insults from distance about my long hair and Oliver's none too subtle aroma of chips. We both looked down at the floor and walked on trying to ignore the laughs. It's so hard going back to this after a week of being treated normally.

Saturday 3rd November

Went to a bonfire with Emily. I went round about four o'clock and it was almost dark. The bonfire was at the local rugby club and we'd been before as they have amazing displays and a massive fire. Emily had to get ready but didn't mind me sitting with her and chatted away laughing at various things but especially at Oliver Oil's thoughts that she might be interested in him. I was relieved. I watched her as she put her makeup on but must've been staring as she turned round and asked if I was ok. I must have blushed and looked away.

Emily said that if I styled my hair and put some makeup on I could probably pass as a girl. I pretended to be horrified at the thought but don't think she believed me. We carried on getting ready but my thoughts were clouded by what she'd said and again I couldn't work out if I was pleased or not. Think I might need to talk to someone about this.

Bonfire and fireworks were great but Emily noticed how quiet I was and apologised about what she'd asked me. I told her that was ok and I wasn't upset just a bit confused. We left it there.

Monday 3rd December

Told mum I wasn't feeling well and wanted to go to the doctors. She made an appointment and when we got there I insisted that I go in on my own as I was at high school and obviously grown up enough. She reluctantly agreed. Inside there was a lady doctor who sat me down and asked what the problem was, all without looking up from her computer screen. I was silent for a few seconds until she scared me by looking straight at me and asking "What?" Don't know why as I should've said something about my thoughts but instead told her I'd hurt my foot and was struggling to walk properly. I took my shoes and socks of and she had a look but couldn't see anything before returning to her computer screen, probably to see if she could fit any more real patients in. She printed off a prescription for mild pain killers and handed it to me before saying to come back and explain what really was the matter. Everyone seems to be able to see straight through me apart from the one person who matters, me.

Left the doctors and mum took me back, though she did ask on the way if I fancied calling in for a hair-cut to at least tidy it up a bit. Was quite relieved when we finally reached school, that mum hadn't asked too many questions about the doctor's and also that Mr Janson hadn't blown up the place in my absence.

Friday 21st December

Broke up for the Christmas holidays. Such a relief that we're to have two weeks off school and relax a bit. Daisy was even more excited as she was going on a residential with school in February up to the Lake District. I was sure this was going to be educational but Daisy seemed more interested in being with her mates away from school and the fun they were going to have. Lake District, February, wet and cold are all words I could think of to do with the trip, fun wasn't one of them. Mum was delighted and immediately told dad he was going to be decorating my room whilst Daisy was away and I could sleep in Daisy's room. Dad mumbled something about not being able to as it was in the middle of the week and he'd be working but mum checked and it was a weekend. Dad went to the pub to try and find a different excuse that would work. When he came back he was slurring his words a bit, didn't have a better excuse and asked where his tea was. Mum told him

it was in the dog. He went to bed slamming the living-

room door leaving us all open mouthed wondering if he'd

left his sense of humour in the bottom of his pint glass.

Tuesday 25th December

Christmas Day. Woke up early hoping I hadn't missed

anything important. Mum and dad were both snoring

but I could hear Daisy tapping away at her laptop

probably chatting away to her friends on some sort of

social media. Don't they ever stop? Pulled the sheets over

my head and tried to block out all the noise and get back

to sleep but couldn't. Eventually got up and wandered

down stairs to get a drink. Father Christmas had been.

Yippee. On days like these it's still nice to think he does exist.

Two hours later mum and dad got up. Mum went straight to the kitchen to try and manoeuvre the turkey into the oven and dad opened a bottle of bubbly in a sort of "I'm helping too" sort of way. He let me and Daisy have a "bucks fizz" which is bubbly and orange juice, and we all raised a glass to "Christmas" and to "that little feller born 2012 years ago today." Think he meant Jesus.

When mum had finished stuffing the turkey into the oven we all opened our presents. Daisy had mainly clothes, mum had jewellery and chocolate, dad had aftershave and socks and I had a mixture of clothes, socks, computer games and books. Think dad had chosen one because it was called "Great haircuts for great lads." Subtle as ever. He laughed when I opened it. He must've been back to the pub to find his sense of humour.

The rest of the day saw us filling our faces with food, especially chocolate, watching repeats from last year and the Queen telling us all what a lovely year we'd had (probably). Wasn't late before we were all tired and went up to bed.

Tuesday 1st January 2013

Can't believe I've been writing this diary for a year now. Just read January 1st last year. This year is a repeat except change the time to 7:45.

Thursday 3rd January

Walked into school this morning and saw Mr McEwan standing at reception looking thoroughly lost. I spoke to him and he told me that he'd changed schools and was going to be teaching maths to Years 7, 8 and 9. Fantastic. He's brilliant and I really miss him from primary. Not just because he knows what he's talking about and is funny, but because he seems to understand us and tries to make sure we're ok and not stressed. Hope he takes us for maths but bet he's teaching the "muppets," as he calls them (those that can do, but can't be bothered).

Friday 4th January

Couldn't believe my luck. Mr McEwan is my new maths teacher (I must be a Muppet ha ha). There was a cheer from all that knew him before and even those that didn't seemed pleased. Maths was going really well, and I don't think he did it deliberately, but Mr McEwan stopped half way through and asked if the classroom was near the kitchens as he could smell chips and it was making him feel hungry. Everyone burst into laughter apart from Oliver who bowed his head and started crying making the ink on his maths book smudge. Mr McEwan couldn't believe what he'd done and apologised to Oliver. I think he may even have shed a tear himself as he wouldn't do anything like that intending to hurt anyone.

Told mum and dad later what had happened and they thought it was hilarious. They can both be so cruel at times, mind you when I got to my room I did see the funny side but think there will be two people who won't be laughing tonight.

Thursday 17th January

Got to school in a really good mood. Since the maths lesson with Mr McEwan mentioning chips, there had been fewer people laughing at my hair but Oliver was being picked on a lot more.

When it was break time I was outside eating a bar of chocolate when a voice told me to give it to him. I looked up and didn't know who it was but he was bigger and stronger than I was. Emily was just passing and told him to get lost but instead he looked at me and punched me hard on the arm and snatched my chocolate away. It hurt loads but I managed to not cry because I knew if I did he'd come back for more another day. He walked off and I asked Emily if she knew who he was and she said his name was Robert the Bruise, a new lad from Scotland who nobody liked and he was in Daisy's year. I thanked her for her help and vowed to keep away from him, or eat my chocolate in private in future.

I told Daisy about what he'd done when I got home but she just laughed when I told her his name. Apparently he'd been expelled from three schools already so it probably wouldn't take long for him to be moving schools again. I just hope that I'm not the reason.

The Holiday Trousers' Diary

Thursday 24th January

Robert has been picking on me for days. There's hardly a day goes by where I don't get another bruise on my arms or body, I certainly know where he gets his name from.

Thursday 31st January

Yet more bruises. He's even started picking on Emily. Had to pluck up courage today to tell a teacher. Spoke to Mr Eagle who just said "It's character building." Well he would say that Robert's good at rugby and in the team so I should've told someone else. I don't want to go back.

The Holiday Trousers' Diary

Monday 4th February

Over the weekend mum noticed the bruises so I told her the story. She went berserk, partly with Robert but mainly with Mr Eagle who doesn't seem to care about pupils just sport. She went into school to complain to the head, Mrs Coldheart and I was called into the head's office to give my side of events. Mrs Coldheart's a nasty woman as she made me feel that it was my fault but fair play to mum she insisted that it wasn't and Robert finished up with a two day exclusion. Safe for a few days now. Slight relief. But worried about what's going to happen when he gets back.

Friday 8th February

Robert back at school and has avoided me. He's still hurting others and the name calling from others has got worse. It's got around that mum came in and I'm now more of a target than I was before. They're calling me names and suggesting I'm gay, probably because I've still not got my hair cut and I'm not great at sport. I don't care!

Who am I kidding? This is killing me!

Thursday 14th February

Daisy off on her trip tomorrow. I'm not sure how I feel. I like Daisy being at school because it feels as though there's always someone to stand up for me and I wish I was going to the Lake District but on the other hand I'm getting my room decorated and I get mum and dad's full attention without Daisy always seeming to interrupt.

Daisy was packing earlier and still insisted on taking sun tan lotion. I had a little giggle about this. It's not sun tan cream she needs, it's waterproofs and E45 cream to repair sore skin from the cold. She had a list of items that she had to take but also insisted on taking a few extra clothes in case they managed to escape for a few hours and go clubbing. She's now 14 and I don't think she'd get in anywhere apart from the nearest youth hostel and I doubt whether that will be buzzing with excitement.

The Holiday Trousers' Diary

Friday 15th February

Daisy left for her trip this morning just as I was moving some of my stuff into her room for the next couple of nights. Dad had taken the day off and was starting to ready my room for its makeover. She looked at me and told me not to touch any of her things before smiling and winking at me. What does she mean? What does she know, or think she knows?

School dragged as usual but could've been worse if I hadn't had the comfort of it being Friday and the tingle of excitement I had of sleeping in a different room. I went to bed early and lay in bed looking round the room at all the things she had in there that were different from my room before putting the light out. I heard mum and dad go to bed early as dad was tired from all the decorating and soon heard them both snoring. I couldn't sleep and so put the light back on and got out of bed. I started looking through her books and the things on her dressing table before deciding to open the wardrobe and have a quick peek. Inside there were loads of dresses and skirts that just looked wonderful in their differing colours. I took out a pink slim fitting skirt and held it up to me and looked in the mirror. For some reason I looked round to see if there was anyone there watching and then slowly stepped into it and pulled it up around my waist. It fitted beautifully and, as like the dress before, felt so good. I could see in the mirror that I was blushing, but at this point I didn't care. I looked further and found a blouse that I thought would go well with the skirt and put that on. Wow I looked great. I couldn't believe how I was feeling so took them both off and hung

them up as best I could before pulling out a little black

dress with some pink embroidered detailing on the front.

This time I listened to make sure there was still the

sound of snoring from my parent's room before pulling

it on. This time there was a zip up the back which I

eventually managed to pull up. I stood there looking at

myself knowing what I was doing was wrong, or at least

not conforming to the usual, but strangely again I

didn't care. Something inside me was telling me this is

how I should be dressing. I don't know how long I stood

there for, but eventually realised I had to take it off.

Getting the zip down again was really difficult but I

managed it and rehung the dress carefully in Daisy's

wardrobe. My heart was beating quickly and I knew

sleep wasn't going to come soon. My mind was racing at what it all meant but deep down I think I knew.

Saturday 16th February

Woke up this morning and the first thing I remembered was wearing Daisy's clothes. I should have felt embarrassed or at least ashamed, but I didn't.

Dad was already decorating so I popped my head round to see how he was getting on. I couldn't quite believe what I saw. He'd decorated the room in the colours of his favourite football team. I hated it. It really wasn't me. Hadn't dad realised by now that I wasn't remotely interested in football. He saw my face and knew I wasn't impressed. He wasn't pleased and said I could've had it in any colour I liked if I'd been paying for it but I assured him it was great. Dad can be so thoughtless at times. Think major fallout avoided, well for now at least.

Mum was making breakfast and promised to take me shopping for some extras for my room. I cheered up at this thought and looked forward to the trip especially as it was just the two of us.

Two hours later we set off for the shopping centre I'd been to with Emily. When we got there the first shop I saw was the dress shop I'd been to before and stared at the window, strange thoughts racing through my head. Mum saw and I made the excuse that I'd seen the dress Emily had bought which seemed to stop her being suspicious. We wandered round for a while before stopping for lunch making this the first purchase of the day. Lunch over we managed to find a few things, a picture of a wrestler, a "this room belongs to" sign and a poster of the periodic table that I thought would please mum but don't think she really believed me and kept asking if I was sure. Well no I wasn't but I could hardly tell her what I thought I wanted when I wasn't really sure myself.

Dad was impressed with what I'd chosen and vowed to finish the room by the time Daisy returned tomorrow. He said he had a surprise for me. I couldn't wait.

Went to bed early again eager to try on some more of Daisy's clothes. As soon as mum and dad were asleep I opened the wardrobe, my heart racing. I tried on three dresses and four skirts before deciding I'd had enough and went to bed. I lay there thinking about my feelings and realised that I didn't really want to be a boy, I just wasn't cut out for it. How then was I going to be a girl or was it going to be my secret for ever and was I going to live a double life? Whatever I chose there were implications for me and my family. For now I wasn't going to do anything because I didn't know what to do. I wasn't going to tell anyone and I was going to try and be more boyish. There, that'll solve it.

Sunday 17th February

Daisy got back from her trip. Me and mum picked her up from school. When the coach arrived back and the doors opened it was like a tidal wave of wet, dirty, smelly teenagers surging out onto the pavement and being hugged by parents. Daisy looked quite glum and hadn't tanned at all though she did look tired, obviously she'd been up all night in the Lake District night spots ha ha. On the way home she started to tell us about the trip and how they'd walked miles in the rain to look at different geographical features which didn't look quite as good in real life as they do in a book. Strange, I thought it'd be the other way round. Once home she stomped upstairs and went straight into the bathroom, locking the door. I went into my room to see how dad was getting on and had the shock of my life. He'd written "Arse" across one wall. I asked him what he was doing and apparently he was writing Arsenal and had mistaken his mm and cm therefore running out of space. I started to laugh and mum came in. She looked at the wall and called dad something I don't want to write. Steam appeared to come out of his ears and he stomped down stairs and opened a beer before slamming the door and going to stand in the garden.

A couple of hours later dad had painted over his Arse and my room was finished. We'd all had a good laugh by then, even dad who'd calmed down. Furniture back in place and new purchases hung I looked round. Now I was being more of a boy I loved it.

No I didn't.

Monday 18th February

Got up and ready for school only for mum to come in and remind me that it was half term. In all the excitement of Daisy's trip and my room being decorated I'd forgotten. Mega.

Mum explained that she had to go to work but Daisy would be looking after me for the day and if we had any problems we were to phone her straight away. I hoped that this wouldn't be needed. I sat downstairs and watched morning telly. Breakfast TV was ok but this was followed by a man shouting at people who were lying and then making them take a test to check if they were lying. He was very aggressive and I didn't feel comfortable watching it, but I did. I suppose that's what they want. That finished I watched a programme about a zoo which was good before starting to watch the antiques programmes marathon that seems to dominate daytime.

The Holiday Trousers' Diary

Daisy came down at 11:30 seemingly in a better mood than yesterday and started to tell me all the gossip from the trip. Robert the Bruise had punched a teacher and had to be fetched by his parents. It was unlikely that he was to return to school ever. This day was getting better by the minute. She then stunned me by asking if I'd enjoyed trying on her clothes. I thought I'd been really careful. Of course I denied it but she didn't believe me and assured me that it was ok and she wasn't cross. I didn't know what to do and blamed mum for moving things in her wardrobe. Eventually she gave up. That was a close one.

Wednesday 20th February

The Holiday Trousers' Diary

Have done homework for the last two days and I've had enough. Decided I needed to do something completely different as can't go out because mum's at work and the weather is terrible. Asked Daisy what I could do and she suggested I do some baking. I'd never cooked anything before so we made a sponge cake together. It was really fun but not sure how we managed to cover most of the kitchen in flour. We were really proud of our cake. Mum thought it looked lovely but dad laughed before asking if we'd washed our hands before making it. Of course we had, well sometime during the day anyway. After tea we all tried a piece. It was ok but not great. Even Arthur left his bit that dad sneaked under the table to give him. Mum wasn't impressed with dad and she kept giving him the evils. Think he'll be buying chocolate again.

AUTHOR - N E SYKES

The Holiday Trousers' Diary

Monday 25th February

Back at school and I was relieved to discover that the rumours of Robert the Bruise being expelled were correct, and the general mood of all the children certainly seemed to have lifted, apart from the boys in the rugby team who'd lost their flanker, at least I think that's what they said. One less thing to worry about. Oliver came to school and surprised us all by not smelling of chips, he now smelled of cabbage. Not sure which I prefer. I must find out if this is an aftershave or deodorant and make sure I never buy any - ever. Emily was really happy and was eager to catch up as we hadn't really spoken during the holidays. She told me that her mum and dad had booked a cruise round the Med for the summer holidays and she couldn't wait to go. It sounded good apart from the worry about sea sickness and not being able to escape anywhere to have time on your own. Bit like home really without the sea sickness.

Rest of the day passed without anything to get excited about apart from home time when we were given pupil information sheets to take home and have checked by our parents to make sure that the contact details etc. were all correct. Simple Simon looked at his and said loudly "it says here I'm a Christian, I'm not I'm Welsh." There was a couple of seconds of silence before we all laughed loudly, even the teacher, before the bell rang and Simon was spared anymore embarrassment.

The Holiday Trousers' Diary

Tuesday 5th March

Panic in school as the teachers told us we'd had "the call" and Ofsted would be here tomorrow for two days. Surely it's not that scary? Mrs Coldheart visited each classroom and barked at all the teachers before instructing them all to make sure they were teaching properly otherwise there'd be problems. What a lovely woman! Remind me to never be a teacher. Mr Eagle looked very worried and mopped sweat off the top of his head and in the sunlight it looked like he'd polished it. Strange how even the toughest and meanest teachers can be scared of such a small word, Ofsted. Next lesson was with Mr McEwan who said in years gone by schools had been given a week's notice which had given them time to make sure everything was perfect and even the worst trouble causers were made to stay away (that's the kids not the teachers). Now though these children had to be hidden away in rooms where Ofsted wouldn't visit. Hope our school has a massive room spare for the next couple of days.

Each lesson for the rest of the day was made up of reading text books and discussing work between ourselves whilst the teachers caught up with their marking. We were all given letters at the end of the day explaining to our parents what was happening and a reminder that we had to be on our best behaviour and try our best to answer questions in class and look like we were learning something. Somehow I felt nervous and it wasn't me being inspected.

The Holiday Trousers' Diary

Wednesday 6th March

Felt troubled last night and wanted something to take my mind off school so dug out the trousers I bought in Spain. Had forgotten how lovely they were as I was trying to be more boyish. Waited till I went to bed and put them on. They were great and the feelings of wearing something completely right really took my mind off the following day and I slept well. Woke up and forgot I had them on and bumped into Daisy outside the bathroom. She looked at me and smiled saying how lovely they looked. Dad saw me too and said he thought I'd got rid of them and they looked ridiculous. Not the start I wanted.

The Holiday Trousers' Diary

Got to school and thought I'd walked into the wrong place. We were all greeted by smiling teachers who were being nice to us and telling us to have a nice day. Felt like we'd walked into an American nightmare. I looked around and spotted some new faces who were holding clipboards and making notes, probably inspectors, though I'd half expected them to have horns growing out their heads the way they'd struck panic into the staff yesterday. They can't possibly think that this is how it is usually!

Mr Eagle had polished his head but there were beads of sweat appearing again even though it was a cold day. He'd even ditched the tracksuit and was wearing a shirt and tie, but the shirt was a little tight and it only looked a matter of time before the buttons burst open like the

Incredible Hulk. Mr McEwan looked his usual smart self but was obviously nervous and hurried away trying to keep out the way of the visitors, probably looking to join the trouble makers in the hidden classroom in the school. Mrs Coldheart walked through with a very tall gentleman laughing and joking with him trying to charm her way to a good grade. Doubt that's going to happen.

It wasn't until after lunch that an inspector visited our classroom. She came in without looking at the children or teacher and plonked herself down in the spare seat next to Oliver. They were just in front of me and I could see her writing notes before looking up and listening to what was being said. After a couple of minutes I saw her turn her head slightly towards Oliver and gently wrinkle her nose. Obviously the aromas of chips and cabbage had caught her attention. She turned her head back again, made a few more notes and decided it was a good time to walk round the class, talk to the children and look at their work. After a few minutes she walked to the door and left, casually looking back at Oliver and then closing the door. Inside the room there was a huge sigh of relief after the teacher had checked she'd gone and then he slumped down in his chair and congratulated us on not shouting out or starting to fight, not that it happens all that often (the fighting).

When we left school we didn't expect to see them but they were there again chatting to some of the parents who were outside. I'm not sure what had been said but there was a group of parents who had surrounded one of the inspectors and at one point I feared for his life they looked so cross.

During tea mum and dad questioned me and Daisy about the day and what had happened. Mum hoped it had gone well but dad said he hoped all the staff would get sacked because they didn't know what they were doing and ought to get proper jobs without such long holidays. He's really grumpy these days and never has any respect for others. I think these teachers do a great job under very difficult conditions, though they do get good holidays.

Went to bed early. Daisy heard me go into my room and poked her head round the door. She asked if I was going to wear those trousers again and to ignore dad as he was a Neanderthal. I love my sister sometimes and felt a bit happier.

Thursday 7th March

After I'd gone to bed last night I decided to pray. I don't go to church but thought I'd give it a go anyway. I asked that when I woke up I'd either a) be a girl or b) be more boyish and not have any thoughts about being a girl. It didn't work. Maybe He was having a night off. I'll try again another night. I got out of bed and this time took my colourful trousers off and put on my pyjamas before going to the bathroom. Didn't meet anyone on the landing. Typical.

The Holiday Trousers' Diary

Got to school and it looked like it was going to be a repeat of yesterday but I was lucky and no inspectors came into my classes. I suppose they talk to each other in the hotel at night and they'd been warned about Oliver and his rather nasty smell. Oh well, small mercies. I bet all the teachers will want to teach him next time they come back to see us.

At the end of the day the staff were back to usual, well when I say usual I mean they were nowhere to be seen, apart from Mr Eagle who was now back in his tracksuit with his shirt hanging up waiting for the next inspection and hoping he hadn't put on any more weight. According to Daisy only one of his buttons had popped off his shirt to howls of laughter, whilst he was explaining what an oxbow lake was during a geography lesson, luckily the inspector had just left the room.

Got home and slumped on the bed. Traumatic week at school and my prayer had been ignored. Decided I had to come up with a solution as this trying to be more boyish strategy wasn't really working. I started to cry until I heard dad come in and shout upstairs to see if I was in. I couldn't let him see me like this. I couldn't talk to him. Who could I talk to and what would they be able to say? Decided I had to do this myself, but what?

Saturday 9th March

Saturdays are always the same. Mum and dad sleep in, Arthur scratches at my door early in the morning to be let out and Daisy asks to go out shopping with her friends. Today was different. Mum and dad still slept in and Arthur scratched at my door but Daisy asked me if I fancied going shopping with her. We asked mum when she eventually got up and she agreed to take us into town for a couple of hours and then she'd pick us up.

She dropped us off at 11:30 and told us where to be at 1:30 and if we weren't there we wouldn't be allowed out again for a long time. Pressure on. First we went into a coffee shop and had a drink and a sandwich which mum had given us the money for. We both felt really grown up. Daisy asked where I fancied going but I wasn't sure and said she could decide. We left "Better Latte Than Never" and headed for the department store. Daisy suggested we start on the ground floor where all the makeup was. I followed her as she looked round before she stopped and started asking me what I thought of this or that colour lipstick. I pointed out a colour called "Really Red Rocks" that I thought she'd like but Daisy wasn't keen so we moved on. Upstairs Daisy started looking at clothes and again I felt drawn to them but pretended I wasn't bothered and suggested we moved on somewhere else. We spent ages looking at different shops and we had a great time chatting about school, friends, family and telly before realising our time was nearly up and mum would be here soon to collect us. When we jumped into the car we were still talking and giggling and sat in the back seat being chauffeured home. It was a lovely day but unfortunately the rest of Saturday wasn't quite as much fun and so I finished up going to bed early feeling a little deflated.

Monday 11th March

Monday morning and back to school. No teachers to welcome us in with their false smiles and Mrs Coldheart returning to being invisible like the entertainment in "Made in Chelsea." First lesson of the day was English with a very grumpy Mr Shakespeare (yes really) who had a terrible case of the Monday morning blues and dished out punishments to anyone who spoke out of turn. French, geography, history and woodwork were all the same before it dawned on me that it was probably Ofsted that had caused this rather than Monday. I started to fear what would happen in school in the next few months. Dad had said that if the report was poor the management would kick out all the useless teachers and replace them with another set of useless teachers because it made it look like the school was doing something about Ofsted's recommendations. We have some great teachers and I just hoped they'd be ok, but at the same time hoped Mr Eagle would be set free.

For tea we had fajitas but the chicken tasted a bit odd until mum told us that she'd been talking to Emily's mum and she had decided to have a go at being part vegetarian and so this was some sort of chicken alternative, probably made of rubber going by the taste. I'm not quite sure what she meant by part vegetarian as at least three quarters of all our meals are non meat already, but I thought I'd wait and see how she got on.

Thursday 14th March

Mum picked me and Daisy up from school and took us straight to the supermarket for a "big shop." This took longer than usual as we had to look at each and every product to see if there was any meat or animal derivatives in the food. She's really going for it but if she keeps it up I'll be very surprised. By the time we got to the checkout the trolley was bursting with soya, tofu, lentils and other products we didn't know anything about, apart from their lack of meat. Mum was in a good mood so Daisy asked her if she could go into town tomorrow with her mates instead of waiting to ask on Saturday morning when mum might be in one of her hung over Saturday strops. Amazingly mum said yes but again there were time limits set and Daisy promised to keep to them. I wasn't invited this time.

Tea was an adventure. But not in a good way. Mum made a tofu curry. I'm glad she told us all otherwise I'd have been worried about the bathroom sponge going missing, it tasted that bad. After we'd eaten, well left it all, mum threw a frozen pepperoni pizza into the oven which was devoured by all, even mum, within a few minutes of being placed on the table. Being vegetarian wasn't going to be as easy for her as it sounded, but being part veggie maybe wasn't too hard. Think she might need a few more tips from Emily's mum.

The Holiday Trousers' Diary

Saturday 16th March

Dad dragged me to the football where I spent an enjoyable hour and a half laughing at the inventive football chants from the crowd. Not sure what the score was at the end but suspect his team didn't score because I don't remember him jumping out of his seat to cheer but do recall the opposite fans waving their scarves around a few times. Silence all the way home, even the radio wasn't turned on to hear the other scores. Probably too painful. I just hope he decides it's not worth going again so I don't have to endure any more Saturday afternoons pretending to enjoy myself.

When we got home mum was cooking a lentil casserole with veg. Yum, just what I was looking forward to. Could the day get any worse? At least Daisy was happy after her trip to town and smiled at me as she clutched her bag of shopping and went up to her room. She called down a few minutes later and said she'd had a burger out so didn't want any tea so I could have hers as well. Yes, the day could get worse, especially when I tasted it. Went to bed hungry.

Thursday 4thApril

Mum has at last abandoned cooking only vegetarian food as she's found she's not very good at it. Dad is even grumpier than usual though hope this news makes him happier. It's my birthday in six days and we're on holiday from school. Dad asked if I'd like to go and watch the football but pretended I'd arranged to meet some friends. He laughed and said I hadn't got any apart from Emily. He's horrible sometimes. He then asked if there was anything special I'd like to do. Not go to the football was my first thought. Shopping with Daisy and Emily was my second, but I was struggling with a suggestion dad would like and think proper boyish. I told him I'd give it a thought and I'd let him know. Went up to my room and played a computer game but my heart wasn't in it because I was trying to think of something special to do that would keep my parents happy, if not me.

The Holiday Trousers' Diary

Friday 5th April

Woke up quite excited. No school tomorrow and I'd decided I wanted to go and see the new "mega smash hit monster trucks in space" movie and then out for tea at a burger restaurant with the family and Emily (but not Arthur). There, definitely very boyish. Dad smiled when I suggested it to him and he agreed it was a great idea, but did I still fancy going to the footie on Saturday as well. Arrrrrgggggghhhh.

Sunday 7th April

Sundays were never really exciting and often the only thing to look forward to was seeing if mum's Yorkshire puddings had risen. They didn't very often and usually had a very heavy doughy texture. But at least she tried, and refused to buy the frozen ones with a picture of a nice old lady on the side who had obviously worked out the perfect recipe. Today was not a surprise as the puds had risen nearly a centimetre before shrinking back to pancake size as soon as they were put on the plate. Mum blamed that nice Irish chef on telly yesterday who had described the fool proof way of making Yorkshire's rise and be as light as a feather but had obviously lied. Maybe next time.

Tuesday 9th April

My birthday tomorrow. Can't wait. We're all going to the cinema and then out for tea. A real treat as the food at home recently hasn't been good. Mum's still telling us all that being veggie is more healthy, however, she's still eating meat and has decided that maybe she should do it in phases and start by cutting out lamb. We never eat lamb anyway so not sure she's really that committed.

Emily texted to say she was looking forward to tomorrow and said I was going to love my present. She didn't give any more clues and I can't think what it'll be. Spent the rest of the day watching an old black and white film on telly followed by countless quiz shows that tempted you into winning a big cash prize if you texted the answer to a question. These questions were rubbish and I think the TV companies underestimate how clever the UK population is. One question asked "who is our head of state?" "Is it A) the Queen, B) Piers Morgan or C) Peppa

Pig?" I know who'd like to be, but don't think the Queen

or Peppa Pig would be too chuffed if Piers Morgan was

the answer. Daisy had been out at her friend's house and

went upstairs. I could hear paper rustling and the sound

of sticky tape being pulled from a roll. Ah must be my

present being wrapped. She came down stairs and made

a point of smiling at me and telling me I was going to

love the present she'd bought me. Don't know why but

there was just something about that grin but couldn't

work out what.

Wednesday 10th April

Birthday. Walked into the kitchen and there was a

small pile of cards on the table and a present to open.

Mum gave me a big kiss and dad shook my hand. Odd. I opened the cards and was delighted with the money from various relatives that fell out onto the table. Mum and dad had also given me money and said I could go shopping with Daisy to spend it. I then opened the present. It was from Daisy and she'd given me a remote control helicopter that was to only be flown indoors. Great. I took it out and set it up before sending it on its test flight. Arthur leapt out of his basket and started barking and chasing it round the room. It was really funny until he nearly caught it but dad managed to grab it out of his jaws just in time. The rest of the morning was spent gazing at the telly thinking about all the lovely things I could buy and then all the things I'd actually be able to buy.

The Holiday Trousers' Diary

Emily came round about two and handed me a present. I tore the paper off to reveal a beautiful pink and purple long sleeved shirt. It was gorgeous and I put it on straight away. It made me feel very special and delighted that I had such a good friend.

Half an hour later we set off for the cinema. Dad had ordered the tickets and it was a good job as there was a queue a mile long (not really, but it was out the door). We settled down in our seats with huge bags of popcorn each and waited for it to start. It was a good film but some of the special effects didn't look real and I think we all came away a little disappointed. However, at the restaurant, the food was fabulous. I had a double burger with special barbecue sauce, chips and salad. It must have been six inches tall and there was no way anyone would ever get their mouth round it, so I had to use my knife and fork to eat it. Everyone else's was the same and it seemed to take ages before we'd all finished. We all sat there feeling really full but when the waitress asked us if we'd like pudding, we still had a look. They were all so tempting so we had three puddings between us and shared them. I shared with Emily, Daisy shared with mum and dad shared with himself. When we left we felt we could hardly walk but managed to get back to the car and set off, dropping Emily at home on the way. So far the day had been brilliant.

When we got back we sat and chatted for a while before Daisy decided it was time for bed. I stayed down to get a drink and then went upstairs. When I got into my room I noticed a small wrapped present on my bed with a little card. It was a box about three inches long and quite narrow. I really didn't know what it could be. When I unwrapped it there was a lipstick in the box called "Really Red Rocks." The one I'd pointed out to Daisy last month. I opened the card and read "thought you'd like this, it'll make you look better when you wear my clothes." I gulped. Daisy hadn't believed what I'd said. I didn't know what to think and just sat on my bed looking at it and wondering whether I should A) cry, B) go and shout at Daisy or C) laugh it off and throw it away. Not so easy this one, so I chose D, be secretly pleased and keep it. I pulled the top off and heard a "plop" sound before twisting the base watching it rise up out the tube and shine in the light of my bedside lamp. It looked gorgeous, I loved the colour and couldn't wait to try it on. But how could I? I then started to cry, but they weren't tears of sadness, they were tears of fear. Fear for what was going to happen when people found out. Fears of what others would say to mum and dad. Fears, because I realised that this is what I wanted.

Daisy came into the room and saw me. She came and gave me a hug and apologised for getting it all wrong and upsetting me. I hugged her back and told her she hadn't. Again she smiled at me and said "good, I've always wanted a little sister." I smiled back at her through the tears but told her not to tell mum and dad, I'd do that sometime when I was ready.

Strange how some days turn out.

The Holiday Trousers' Diary

Friday 12th April

Good Friday. Great Friday actually. Dad went to the football and didn't take me. Mum met some work colleagues for lunch and a drink and left Daisy at home looking after me. We chatted for a while about nothing in particular before she brought up the subject of me trying on her clothes. I told her I'd been having these feelings on and off for the last couple of years and hadn't felt like I fitted in properly but had tried to hide and ignore them hoping they'd go away but when Daisy had gone with school to the Lakes the temptation had been too much and I realised that I felt right when wearing them. She was sympathetic and explained that her and Emily had both guessed there was something I was hiding and they suspected that this was it but there hadn't been proof until then. I couldn't quite believe that my sister had been talking to my best friend about me for ages and hadn't said anything. She then asked if I'd tried my lipstick out, which of course I hadn't. This pleased her and she sent me to go and get it whilst she got one of hers. She then showed me how to put it on and I followed. It was very embarrassing and I felt very self-conscious but looking in the mirror I thought it looked fabulous. Daisy squealed with delight and told me how beautiful I looked. She then decided to do all my hair and make-up saying that if anyone came back she'd say she made me be her model to practice on. I loved it and when she finished I hardly recognised myself. I could feel my heart beating rapidly and this only speeded up when Daisy suggested I put on one of her dresses and I could choose. We opened the wardrobe and chatted about each one deciding whether it would look right with the make-up. When we came to the one like Emily had bought the time I went shopping with her my mind was set and we both agreed that this was a good choice, plus I'd already tried it on before and knew it fitted well. Daisy helped me put it on and straighten it so it looked right and then gave me a pair of black shiny shoes with a highish heel to complete the outfit. She said I looked wonderful. Looking in the mirror nearly took my breath away as I turned and posed to look at myself from different angles and any lingering doubts about whether this was what was right for me vanished. There was definitely no doubt at all. I wore the dress, shoes and makeup for the next couple of hours enjoying the swish of the skirt and the freedom I felt, practicing walking and sitting correctly, before Daisy reminded me that dad would be home soon and so I quickly changed back into my usual clothes. Once back as a boy I felt very flat and boring and so began to cry again. I was getting good at this. I think life is going to be very different.

Saturday 13th April

Couldn't quite work out what today was like. My head was spinning from what had happened the last two or three days, especially the fact that at last I had confided in my sister, even though she already knew and this made me happy but nervous and relieved but anxious. My emotions swung from happy one minute to feelings of being quite depressed the next. This hadn't gone unnoticed by my mum and she kept asking if I was ok. Dad hadn't noticed and just sat and read his newspaper occasionally grunting about dishonest politicians and overpaid footballers that didn't know they were born. Emily texted to see if I was ok but I didn't know whether Daisy had told her so lied about what I was doing to try and make it seem like a normal day. I was delighted when it was bed time so I could have a proper think about things and what my plan of action was to be.

Monday 15th April

Haven't made any real decisions over the last few days so I'll wait before I tell mum. We're all off to the seaside for the day on Friday (19th) so that's something to look forward to as long as Arthur behaves himself in the car, unlike last time. Daisy hasn't really spoken to me about the other day yet, I think she can see I need a few days for the whole thing to sink in.

Friday 19th April

Went to the seaside today. Arthur farted several times in the car and dad blamed me each time. He's so funny but I didn't laugh. Mum scowled at him each time and Daisy tutted, but he didn't seem to get the message. Dad suggested we play pub cricket on the way. That's where you score runs for the number of limbs the name of the pub has to a maximum of six. If the name of the pub isn't an animal you're out and the next player starts. He decided this just as we started on the motorway and of course there aren't any pubs on motorways. Again dad thought it funny. Again nobody laughed.

I was having a rubbish day at the beach as I couldn't stop worrying about what had happened recently until Daisy squeezed my hand and whispered that everything was going to be ok and that she was there to help me along the way. Wow, my mood changed instantly and I think I've got the best sister ever.

Monday 13th May

We've been back at school about three weeks. Still not told mum. Still anxious. Still getting ridiculed for my long hair and the name calling is really hurting. Got home from school and went straight to my room and sat on the bed wondering what I'd done to deserve this. Daisy came in holding a small bottle of nail varnish and asked what I thought of the colour. This is the first time she's spoken to me this way in a while. I said it was lovely. She then asked when did I have sport at school? I told her it was today and we didn't have any more until next week, why? Her face beamed and asked if I wanted my toenails painting as I wasn't going to get changed for anything so nobody was going to see, I just have to keep my slippers on at home. I readily agreed and so she got to work. It was a deep burgundy colour and she painted them with great skill. When she'd finished they looked beautiful but what's more I felt great though a little disappointed I couldn't have my fingernails done.

She said at the end that if I liked the colour I ought to get

a lipstick that would go with them as the one I'd got

wouldn't really go. If I wanted she'd take me shopping

again soon and help me spend my birthday money. By

the time bedtime arrived I was already planning the trip

and wondering what else I could buy.

Tuesday 14th May

Tingled with excitement when I got to school. Nobody

knew my little secret inside my socks and shoes and for

once I approached the day more confidently. Nothing to

worry about as no one was going to see them. By the end

of the day I'd forgotten but my confidence had remained

and it was only when I questioned myself that I remembered.

When I got home I went straight to my room and started on my homework. Daisy came in and asked if I was ok and then asked if this Saturday was ok for a trip to town. Was it? Of course it was. Couldn't wait.

Saturday 18th May

Saturday at last and shopping day with Daisy. We were due to leave at 11 but just before, Emily arrived and came in. I told her that I was just going shopping with Daisy and she said she knew and that Daisy had asked her if she'd like to come too. I went up to my room to finish getting ready and asked Daisy why? She then told me that she'd confirmed to Emily about my dressing as a girl but had sworn her to secrecy. I couldn't believe it and started to cry again (this is getting a habit), I believed this was our secret and the thought of someone else knowing was just too frightening. Daisy assured me that Emily wouldn't tell anyone. I reminded her that that's what she said.

Emily came upstairs to see if everything was ok and saw my red eyes and guessed that I now knew. She put her arms round me and gave me a hug telling me that she'd suspected for ages but wasn't 100% sure and had asked Daisy, who then confirmed it, but that everything was ok and it wouldn't change our friendship. I looked into her eyes and knew she was telling the truth. Maybe this was good. I hope so.

We eventually set off for town and headed straight for

the department store where Emily and Daisy both started

looking for makeup for me to spend my money on. Of

course I had to agree but they talked as though they were

buying it so that none of the sales assistants became

suspicious. They (1) bought a couple of lipsticks, an eye

shadow set and some foundation before moving on to the

clothes section where they picked out two skirts, a dress

and a blouse which Daisy tried on knowing they'd fit

me as we are both the same size. After three hours of

shopping and giggling I decided I needed to spend some

of my birthday money on something boyish so as not to

raise eyebrows when we got home so bought a football

shirt that I'd probably never wear. By the end of the day I

felt great and can honestly say I'd had one of the best

shopping trips ever. I couldn't wait to try it all on but knew that I'd have to wait for the right time when mum and dad were both out.

Monday 20th May

PE at school. I'd forgotten to remove the nail varnish. All the boys laughed at me and called me a gay boy and a poof. I laughed it off and told them that my sister had played a trick on me when I fell asleep and had then hidden the nail varnish remover. Got punched by two of the boys and threatened. Nobody wanted to be my PE partner and there were laughs and sneers every time my name was mentioned. When the teacher asked what was going on I had to lie and say there wasn't a problem and that the other boys were just having a joke. Don't think I can carry on with this. My life at school is hell and apart from Emily and Daisy I can't talk to anyone. Why am I like this? Why couldn't God just make me normal?

When I got home I told Daisy she could keep the stuff we'd bought and I didn't want anything to do with it. From now on I'm going to be normal!

Friday 26th July

Broke up from school today for the summer holidays. School has been a nightmare since that day in May but at least the bullying eased off a bit towards the end and

I won't get punched, name called or verbally abused for at least six weeks. Being a normal boy has got me through school but has been hell in my own head. I wish I knew what to do and how to handle this because I don't feel that I can carry on this way. I have to make a decision and deep down I know whichever one it is it'll hurt, either me or my parents or probably both.

Thursday 8th August

On holiday in Spain for two weeks and having to share a room with Daisy again. Not easy and it's really brought those feelings of being in the wrong body again to the front of my mind seeing all of her stuff in front of me and beginning to feel jealous. Daisy has been great and hasn't talked about it since that day but she could tell something wasn't right. We talked for ages into the night and she said she'd stick with whatever decision I made but if I decided on the girl route I'd have to tell mum because if I didn't she'd find out anyway. I struggled to sleep. I knew what the right choice was but I didn't know whether I'd be brave enough to follow it through.

Monday 12th August

We all went out for a lovely meal tonight. Well it was until dad disagreed with something mum said about the amount he was drinking and he then went off to find a different bar away from her nagging. We all sat there a little shaken by his sudden temper eruption and walk out. Mum was very quiet for a while and just looked down at her plate before suddenly looking up and smiling at us both and telling us not to worry as dad had a lot on his plate at the moment and was a little stressed. I looked over at his plate and it was empty as dad rarely left anything at meal times usually "hoovering" everything up that was left. Mum laughed when she saw my face and explained it was nothing to do with food. I asked what he was worried about and she said work. Mum said she wasn't worried about work but did have concerns about me and Daisy and wondered if we were both happy. Daisy said she was and then looked at me. I don't know why, and I suppose there can never be a perfect time, but I blurted out to mum about dressing as a girl, being bullied and just being very confused with life before starting to cry again. There was silence for what seemed like ages before she told me that she knew there was something, and she'd known since I was tiny, but couldn't quite work out what. She put her hand on mine and assured me that she understood. This made me feel relieved so I told her about the clothes and makeup I'd bought and how Daisy had helped me and what had happened at school. Mum frowned and looked rather disappointed that I'd not confided in her before. Maybe for a first confession I'd perhaps said too much. Silence ensued apart from mum paying the bill and we walked quietly back to the hotel. Once outside our room mum gave me the biggest hug I can remember and said we'd speak again and that everything would be ok, but not to tell dad, she'd do that all in good time depending on what my decision was going to be.

By the time I got into bed I felt that by telling mum, I'd already made the decision. As we were dropping off to sleep I think Daisy called me her little sister again. Confirmation.

Tuesday 13th August

We were woken by the sound of mum shouting at dad. Shirking responsibility, childish, grow up and hangover were all words we could hear before tears (both), silence and sorry. Not the best way to start a day on holiday.

When we went down for breakfast we all tucked into large plates of pastries followed by sausages and beans except dad who ordered two large paracetamol and a glass of water. Serves him right. Dad went for a lie down after apologising to us all for walking off and mum took us into town to look at the shops. I was amazed at the difference our conversation had from the previous night because when we went into clothes shops I was asked whether I liked them and it was almost like mum had accepted my transformation. She was probably just testing to see if I was genuine but I started to feel good about myself again for the first time in a while. Later we went for a drink on the seafront and watched the world go by. There are some strange people out there, me included I suppose, but we all laughed at English sock and sandal wearing men, milk bottle white skin with bright red vest shaped sunburn and huge bellies that must have cost a fortune to grow. Bad start to the day but we ended up closer, apart from dad who was probably still asleep.

Friday 23rd August

Back home and those feelings of insecurity and dread are back. I wish I could just disappear and become me without all this difficulty.

Dad went to work and mum stayed home and sat me down. She explained that she wanted to help but really didn't know what to do. She also mentioned that she still hadn't told dad and was a little worried about what his reaction would be. We looked at the internet to see what we should do. Cute cats and puppies falling over and chasing their own tails made us smile but didn't help. We then got serious and quickly realised that we should consult a doctor. More dread. I hope it's not the one I went to see before because she seemed more interested in her computer screen than she did in me. Mum said she'd get an appointment if I was really serious. I was, but asked her to delay a little so I could build up the courage.

Monday 2nd December

How have we got here so quickly? School has been bearable, just, and home has been great. I've been dressing as a girl when dad's been out and mum has accepted this but still not told him. Daisy and Emily have been true to their word and not told anyone but realise the time is coming that I need to go to the doctors and sort something out. Also, dad needs to be told but nobody at home seems to have the guts to do it. Mum has booked an appointment for this Friday (6th) and is going with me. Dad thinks I've got a verruca so isn't suspicious.

Friday 6th December

D day. I was so nervous when I got up I could hardly eat my cereal. Arthur sat under the table and licked my feet which dad noticed and chased him away saying the last thing we needed was a dog with a verruca on his tongue (is that really a thing?). Felt really sorry for Arthur as he hasn't a clue, hasn't done anything wrong and has been shouted at.

Dad went to work and mumbled something about the doctor prescribing me a haircut as well as verruca treatment. What's he going to say when he finds out the truth?

Silence in the car on the way to the doctor's. We walked in and were immediately questioned by the receptionist what the appointment was for. Mum told her it was private and then asked if she "questioned everyone because she had to" or "was she just a nosy cow?" Not the best start. After about 20 minutes we were called in and to my horror it was the same doctor as before. Again she didn't look up from her screen but waived her hand motioning us to sit down. A few seconds later her chair swivelled round, she smiled and asked us what the problem was. I went to speak but my mouth became dryer than the Arizona Desert and all I could do was croak. She pounced on this thinking that was the problem until mum stopped her and explained what we were really there for. Mum was great and to be fair so was the doctor as she turned to talk to me with a concerned look on her face rather than the howls of laughter I'd dreamt of the night before. Apparently this is called gender dysphoria which she explained was becoming more common which was causing problems in itself as there was now up to a two year waiting list to see a professional at a Gender Identity Clinic who could help but she would refer me and I'd hear in due course.

Mum asked a few more questions but I was now feeling rather dazed and didn't hear what they were. TWO YEARS? How was I going to survive another two years? What was I going to do?

Wednesday 25th December

Christmas day and the smallest pile of official presents I've ever seen downstairs but a much larger pile of secret (away from dad) presents in my room. Mum, Daisy and Emily had all bought me two, a boy present and a girl present. Dad still doesn't know and seems more interested in what's in a bottle than what we're up to. I opened the official gifts and must now be quite a good actor as dad looked pleased as he'd chosen a couple, a picture of Wembley and some deodorant that attracts hoards of women when any man wears it, perfect. Upstairs after the formalities of the downstairs present opening I looked at my other pile of gifts. They were wonderful. Makeup, clothes and jewellery. I was delighted and couldn't wait to try them on but knew I had to wait until the effects of food and alcohol sent dad to sleep for a couple of hours.

Just after Channel 4's alternative Christmas message dad started to snore loudly and I knew I could be me. I went upstairs and tried on my presents. They were great and mum and Daisy both agreed that I certainly looked beautiful and that being a girl was the right choice. They could see how happy I looked as a girl and how miserable I looked as a boy. I asked mum when she was going to tell dad and she said that she'd do it on New Year's Day. A fresh start and all that. My heart sank but I knew it had to be done. Dad had to know and I had to be me more often than I was now.

Wednesday 1st January 2014

New year started off pretty much the same as the previous two until dad came down to make a cup of tea for him and mum as well as downing a couple of paracetamol. He ruffled my hair, wished me happy New Year and wandered back upstairs whistling something tuneless, but he seemed to know what it was. Daisy came down and asked if mum had told dad yet? Told her I didn't think so because dad was still in a good mood.

At about midday the first signs of mum telling dad were heard. "Are you havin' a laugh?" were shouted by dad and I think mum started crying. Loud footsteps echoed across the ceiling before stamping down stairs and the kitchen door being flung open. Dad just stood and stared at me. His bristly face seemed to have aged since the turn of the year and the cup of tea and it seemed to take ages before he found his voice. He asked me if it was true that I was a fairy. Hurtful, but I couldn't deny that it would have been nice to play one in the school play. I didn't really know how to reply as I knew what he meant just didn't see it that way myself. I told him that I wasn't but he persisted by asking if I'd been dressing as a girl. Think I went a bit red and just nodded my head. It was at this point Paddy McGuiness would say "let the blue touch paper see the flame" as dad started shouting. Many things. All painful. I didn't quite catch them all but the gist of it all was that if I still wanted to live there I had to stop and be a proper man. When he'd finished there was silence apart from Arthur slurping water out of his bowl totally unaware of the large dad shaped firework that had just gone off in the kitchen. I tried to explain that I didn't want to dress as a girl it was just something I felt I had to, natural even. Dad wasn't listening and started pacing round the room mumbling about how it was mum and Daisy's fault and how could he be to blame, he'd taken me to football matches and bought me manly deodorant at Christmas and I liked those didn't I? No!

Mum came down and told him to go back to bed and have a rest. She tried to say things to make it all better but didn't say them with much conviction. I think even mum was shocked at dad's reaction. She stayed in the kitchen all day trying to make his favourite food and keeping out of his way.

Stayed dressed as a boy for the rest of the day because as much as dad had hurt me I felt that causing him to have a heart attack on January 1st wouldn't be the best way to round off the day. Daisy agreed with me and we actually had a laugh at dad's expense because we'd never heard such language, though we didn't laugh for long as we knew that home would be difficult for all of us, not least me, for a while. By the time I went to bed I felt more miserable than at any time in the last two years.

Thursday 2nd January

Dad's mood hadn't changed. He still had steam coming out of his ears, not literally that would've been weird, but he was still not happy. He sat down at the table and asked what he'd done wrong. I assured him that he hadn't done anything wrong, in fact the football and manly deodorant had helped (I thought this might help) but he managed to take it the wrong way because he thought I meant that it had helped convince me I wanted to be a girl. I can't win. Mum came down soon afterwards looking tired but managed to smile at me and give me a kiss. For a brief second I felt wanted again, before dad asked if it was just a phase I was going through, a bit like collecting Pokemon cards. I explained that I wished it was and I didn't ask for this or indeed want it but I couldn't do anything about it. I went up to my room and texted Emily and told her that my dad now knew and everything else that had happened and been said. She didn't return the text for nearly five minutes and I was beginning to think she'd decided that having a transgender friend wouldn't be good for her image. She was really supportive though and even had a laugh when I mentioned about the football.

Later on that evening dad came into my room and sat on the bed. He tried to talk to me about how he felt and how that was the reason he reacted as he had. He stopped short of saying sorry and never once asked me about me. I cried when he'd gone. Mum heard and came in to see me. She gave me a big hug, told me that dad would come round and he would eventually understand and that he'd had a lot to take in. I smiled at her but didn't feel so sure that it would happen. I'm dreading him seeing me dressed up.

Sunday 5th January

Dad was happy again. His team had won two games since the New Year. One in the league and one in the cup. I decided to get dressed up and just appear in front of him because I thought it would soften the blow as he was in a good mood. Before doing so I asked mum if he was insured to make sure she was looked after if he died of a heart attack. She laughed and said that probably wouldn't happen but yes he was. I went upstairs and put on a blue dress with ¾ sleeves (for some reason decided against pink in case it was too much), just a little makeup and styled my now shoulder length hair using my straighteners. When I walked into the room he did a double take like Tom and Jerry would do, but at least his eyes didn't shoot out and back to the sound of a 1950's American car horn. He looked me up and down and uttered the phrase "bloody hell my son's turned into RuPaul, what are the neighbours going to say?" before grabbing his coat and walking out the front door no doubt going to the pub to see if the answer to his problem son was at the bottom of a glass of beer.

Me, mum and Daisy had a group hug and snivelled into each other's shoulders before standing back and having an embarrassed giggle. Why do people do that? Mum looked me up and down and said how beautiful I looked and then assured me again that everything would be ok with dad. When she's said this before I believed her but this time there seemed to be a hint of doubt in her voice.

Monday 6th January

Back to school. Again. Emily met me at the gate and grabbed my hand and squeezed it hard. She asked if I was ok and up till then I was but then started to blurt out everything that I hadn't already told her and especially last night's events. She looked at me with the same pity you look at a dog who's just appeared on telly with no one wanting to give it a home, in fact I was beginning to feel like that dog and wanted Paul O'Grady to come and rescue me. She told me not to worry and everything would work itself out but, I wasn't so sure.

In school everyone was talking about their Christmas and what they got. I wanted to tell them I'd got a lovely new dress and some make-up but felt that wouldn't go down well and I really didn't need laughing at or being punched today, actually any day.

Mr McEwan was his usual cheerful first day back at school self after the holidays which meant he was grumpy. Obviously he'd not won the lottery again and had to still teach but at least he did smile a few times especially after he heard the news that Mrs Coldheart was going to retire at the end of term, a fact he shared with great delight and there was a loud cheer from one and all. He'd also been opening up crackers over Christmas dinner because he told us a few jokes, none of which were funny. Where that tumble weed came from I don't know.

Rest of the day wasn't too bad. Emily checked in with me at lunch as did Daisy but for once they needn't have worried as for a change I wasn't being picked on.

Friday 10th January

The Holiday Trousers' Diary

After a reasonable week at school dad turned up in the middle of French telling me I had a dentist's appointment. Knew there was something fishy as dad never takes me anywhere apart from football. We sat in the car and set off in silence. Eventually dad said we were going to see someone who could "cure me." Of what? He turned and smiled at me narrowly avoiding knocking a man off his scooter but receiving a blast from his horn as second prize. I decided not to ask and just waited to arrive. When we pulled up it was an old Victorian building with vertical blinds hung in the large front window at an angle so you couldn't see who was in. There was a brass plaque attached to the door which said Dr Angus Throstlby, psychiatrist, next to an intercom which dad pressed. The door clicked open and we made our way through a narrow corridor to be greeted by a pleasant looking lady who smiled at us and took our names before asking us to take a seat. After a few minutes the consulting room door opened and a well-dressed man walked out smiling a toothpaste advert smile, made another appointment and left. Dr Throstlby eventually poked his head out of the room and, after looking down at his notes stared at me and said "James would you like to come through?" James? I hadn't been called that in years. He could see my confusion and checked his notes again but by this time I was on my feet walking towards him. He seemed quite nice and told me to sit down in what looked a really comfy chair but was actually in fact the world's most uncomfortable. We chatted for ages mainly about my home life and how long I'd felt the need to wear a dress before he said our time was up and he'd like a quick word with dad. Me and dad swapped rooms and I sat outside with the woman on reception. She was wearing a lovely deep green skirt and white blouse and had lovely understated make-up on which must have taken her ages to make it look so natural. Dad came out a few minutes later looking cross and marched me out to the car where we set off back to school. I told him I thought the doctor was nice but dad said we weren't going back as it had cost a fortune. Dad thought that one session would be enough to help but apparently this sort of thing would carry on over a number of months and years and at the end there was no guarantee anything would change. He dropped me off at the school gates just as everyone was leaving for the day. Thanks dad.

Saturday 11th January

Dad spent the morning banging all the cupboards shut and shouting at Arthur who eventually lay down under the dining room table shaking. Mum didn't fair much better, though she drew the line at lying under the table. Eventually dad went to the football and left us all in peace. Daisy came downstairs looking like she'd just discovered a cure for all known diseases. She looked at me and smiled then suggested we go shopping somewhere we'd not been to before with me dressed up and mum could take us. I thought it was a great idea as long as mum was happy to take us but at the same time felt scared that someone would recognise me and laugh. School was already bad enough but this could make it ten times worse, not that I could quantify ten times. Mum agreed slightly reluctantly and we all went to get changed with Daisy wearing a skirt and top, mum had trousers and a fleece and I was wearing my best dress with strappy sandals. When they both saw me they agreed it looked good but maybe a little too much for a shopping trip. Daisy took me back upstairs and found a skirt and t-shirt combination with a pair of highish heeled boots before checking my make-up which she thought looked fine.

We left the house all smiles even though I felt sick to the bottom of my stomach, but at least I was with mum and Daisy who'd save me from all the insults I'd probably get. When we arrived at the shopping centre I felt a little better but found myself checking all the other shoppers to see if they were staring at me and laughing. Nobody was. Bit more relaxed. We drifted into one shop after another looking at clothes and make-up and for the very first time I felt completely normal and I was doing what I should. However, there was a problem when I needed the loo. Where was I to go? I whispered this to Daisy who giggled a bit until she realised how worried I was. She grabbed my arm and led me into the ladies saying we'd be fine as I'd be in a cubicle and nobody would know. It was like another world in there. It didn't smell of wee and the toilets had been flushed before the next occupant arrived, although some of the conversations I could hear made me blush a bit.

We finished our shopping and set off home. I felt as happy as I'd ever been. Nobody had laughed or punched me and all the shop assistants had treated me as a girl. Even more confirmation as if I needed it that this was what I wanted/needed.

Dad was home when we got back and met us at the door. His face, already miserable, dropped even further when he saw what I was wearing. He hurried us in and then shouted at mum for encouraging me and saying he'd be the laughing stock of the neighbourhood. HIM, what about me? I cried making my mascara run and Daisy called him a pig. Mum just took it solemn faced before explaining where he'd be sleeping tonight. I may be wrong but don't think he'll fit in the dog basket and Arthur wasn't going to be happy as he'd now have to find somewhere else to sleep.

How are we all going to carry on like this? I feel so guilty, as this is all my fault but I also feel that to be me, the journey has to continue and I'm now powerless to stop it.

Friday 24th January

Went to school as normal after wading through dad's duvet that was littering the floor of the lounge. This has now become normal after his disagreement with mum. He'd tried to be nice to us all but mum wasn't having any of it. Think he's really hurt her this time, though I'm getting used to it.

School had been a chore apart from maths with Mr McEwan who'd made us all laugh when he'd tried to sing the 12 times table to us like at primary school. Well intentioned, but his voice wouldn't be out of place on an X-Factor worst singers contest, in fact he could win. I walked home with Daisy who chatted constantly about her day and who had said what to whom. When we walked in mum was stood there and she'd been crying. She told us dad had left as he couldn't cope with what was going on any more. He really did love us all but found everything too hard and felt he had no choice. Also I'd received a letter from the doctors that said I had been referred for assessment and that the referrals would start in a couple of weeks. Can't believe there'd been a cancellation and I'd somehow managed to shorten the queue by nearly two years. Think this had really been the tipping point and if he did love us/me he'd make more of an effort to understand and help me through it. Can't say I was sorry he'd gone but felt a bit for mum because she'd made him sleep downstairs trying to stand up for me, maybe she'd pushed him too far, maybe he was a narrow minded pillock who didn't have the guts or love to stand up for his son/daughter who needed him. Texted Emily and told her what had happened expecting her to rush over and give me a hug but she was just at Nando's with her mum and dad. That made me feel so much better!

The Holiday Trousers' Diary

Friday 7th February

First session with the psychologist. Mum took me and I was expecting some plush offices in the middle of town. Instead it was a 1960's building with blinds that didn't quite drop down to the bottom of the window with slats that didn't quite open or close at the same angle as the others. Tatty and scruffy are the words I'm looking for. We walked in, gave our names to the woman behind the desk and sat down on chairs that wouldn't have looked out of place on a bonfire. After waiting half an hour and listening to the receptionist whisper to her friend on the phone that she didn't know how she'd got up this morning after getting hammered on shots last night, the door at the far end opened and a short fat man wearing a long white coat called us through. His name was Dr Trevor Sinclair (no relation to the footballer and dad would be proud if he knew I'd written this) who seemed quite nice. However, I couldn't quite concentrate because I kept wondering how he'd get up if he fell over as his stomach was so large. Eventually I started to listen and chat with him about what I'd been through and how I felt. He listened intently, making notes all the time, occasionally asking mum the odd question and nodding his head.

Eventually our time was up and he leaned back in his chair taking off his glasses and placing one of the arms in his mouth and looking at us both. He then told me that he fully understood how I was feeling etc. but in order to move the process on and convince him that this was what I really wanted I had to start living as a girl full time, even when at school. My heart sank. Not the living as a girl full time bit because that's what I wanted but having to do it at school which I felt could be very dangerous.

On the way home from the meeting mum asked me what I wanted to do. I told her that there wasn't really a choice I had to do it. She then said she'd see the head at school and explain the situation then after half term I'd start going to school as a girl. Part of me was excited by this as at last I was doing something completely positive but the fear of being killed by some of the other kids was definitely a worry.

Decision made. Just do it, as the advert says.

The Holiday Trousers' Diary

Sunday 9th February

First visit to dad's new place.

Daisy and I walked up the stairs in an old Victorian house to dad's new flat. There was a smell of mothballs mixed with fried onions and boiled potatoes which didn't give us a lot of confidence that the flat itself would be a luxury pad. We were right. Paint peeled from the walls, ceiling tiles hung down exposing the skeleton frame underneath and the furniture was held together by duct tape and hope. Dad greeted us with a cheery smile and gave us a hug, something he rarely did at home, and started by asking how mum was. If he was so bothered why didn't he phone her? We chatted about nothing for a while before he asked if we'd like to go out for lunch. Of course we both said we would, mainly to get out of the flat, and set off down the stairs. As we got down to the first floor a man appeared from a doorway dressed in dirty pyjamas and carrying a bowl of cat food. He looked at us and shouted "Have you seen my Freddy?" We asked him what he looked like and he said he couldn't remember it was so long since he'd seen him. Another voice came from the flat telling him to come back in as Freddy had died in 1982 and he was to stop pestering other people. The old man looked at us with confusion and asked if we'd seen Freddy. Dad pushed us away saying we hadn't and we trotted quickly down the stairs. Once outside dad ushered us into the car and we set off. Ten minutes later we were sitting in McDonalds. Nice but not really what we had in mind for lunch. The whole place was filled with single dads and their children along with small groups of teenagers trying to look tough by swearing as many times as possible throughout each sentence spoken to each other. Dad apologised as apparently his reservation at the top Italian in town had been double booked and they'd phoned to cancel this morning. Yeah right.

We ate in silence trying not to hear what was going on at the other tables but failing miserably. This was probably the worst most awkward meal I'd ever had anywhere ever.

When we finished we went back to the flat to be depressed even more. We ran up the stairs as quietly as possible past the first floor and the old man and his bowl of cat food up to dad's flat. Once inside I took a deep breath and told him what had been said at the meeting the previous day. He was either trying to avoid the subject or simply didn't know. Personally I think he's an ostrich burying his head in the sand. His reaction was what I expected. He hit the roof dislodging a few more tiles (no, not really) before telling me that I couldn't see him here (or anywhere) if I was dressed as a girl. I walked out with Daisy following close behind. As we got to the door I turned round and explained that this was something I had to do and if he really loved us all he'd have to accept the situation or he'd have to live in this scruffy flat with mad neighbours for quite some time. He didn't reply. I closed the door and we walked downstairs. On the first floor we came across a woman wearing a dirty nighty and carrying a cup of tea and a couple of biscuits. She looked at us and asked if we'd seen an old man looking for a cat. We ran the rest of the way until we got outside.

When we got home we told mum what had happened and what dad's flat was like. She sat there impassive. She'd not said anything since he'd left and it looked like this was to continue.

Monday 10th February

Mum came into school with me today and asked to see the head. We both went in and sat down. Mrs Coldheart listened and kept glancing at me trying to smile and make me feel more comfortable but just managed to scare me a bit. Mum wanted reassurances that I'd be protected from the stone-age children that wouldn't understand what was happening and that the staff would be fully briefed so that they were able to look out for me as well. This she got, but as we left I didn't feel confident at all as there wasn't a great history of children being treated compassionately in this school.

Mum left and I re-joined my lessons but I couldn't concentrate after recent events. Things were moving quickly and the future was beginning to look very scary indeed. Told Emily at break and she squealed in delight grabbing both my hands and telling me that she'd help me get ready and, more importantly stand up for me if any of the other kids had a go. This helped but wasn't sure how she'd fair if I was set on by a group of kids determined to beat me up. Just hope this doesn't happen.

When I got home from school mum told me there was a present on my bed for me. I ran upstairs and flung open the door. There on the bed was my new uniform of blouses, blazer, skirt, tights and even a bra, in fact the only thing missing was a pair of shoes. Mum came in a few minutes later and said we'd get the shoes together as she wasn't sure which I'd prefer and anyway I needed to try them on first. I gave mum a hug and thanked her for being so supportive. She told me she'd always be there for me and help as much as she could and anyway she'd always known this day would come as even from a small child I'd been different from the other boys I'd been with at playschool.

Daisy had her phone face on and wandered in. She asked what was going on without once taking her eyes from the screen. Eventually she looked at my new clothes and smiled but behind that smile I could see that there was also a hint of worry as some of the flack I'd get would be diverted towards her. We still had a group hug though.

Saturday 15th February

School finished yesterday and boy Nicky left without telling anyone only to be replaced by girl Nikki a week on Monday. Today is the first day as a full time girl. Nervous but excited.

Mum came into my room just as I'd finished getting dressed and said how lovely I looked. Then to make things even better she explained that dad couldn't see us this weekend as he'd had an accident on the stairs at his flat involving a bowl of cat food and a cup of tea and he'd sprained his ankle and couldn't walk for a few days. I giggled a bit at that but then realised he's still my dad and I shouldn't think that way. Still pleased mind.

Later on we went to buy some school shoes and after the last trip I felt more confident of going out. We arrived and walked in peering in the shop windows and deciding what we'd like to buy if we had the money until I caught the faint aroma of chips and knew that Oliver was standing close to me. I turned slowly to look round and saw him about five feet away staring at me. It was obvious he knew who I was because I was with Daisy. "Hello" he said, "Why are you dressed like that?" I explained to him why and that from now on this was how I was going to dress even at school. A sly grin formed on his face and he said "Well done, good luck" before hastily turning round and wandering off. As reactions go this could've been worse.

We got some new shoes which weren't that dissimilar to the shoes I'd been wearing, before setting off home. When we got back one of the neighbours stopped mum and asked her some question about drains. I'm pretty sure that she didn't really want to know about drains it was more to see what was going on with me dressed like I was. By the look on her face she wasn't impressed but didn't say anything, however, she almost ran back home probably to tell the rest of the family about the strange boy/girl next door. I'm going to have to get used to this for a time before everyone realises what's going on and that this is who I really am.

Sunday 16th February

Was woken by my phone telling me I'd got a new message. Now to most people that's something that happens every day but for me it only happened when Emily sent me a message as I didn't have any other friends. Looked at the time (8:30) and clicked open the message. It was a friend request on my social media page from Oliver. Wasn't sure whether to accept or not but did anyway. Then in the space of twenty minutes there were another eight requests. What was going on? Then the messages started to arrive. Gay, puff, nancy boy, sissy, tranny, woofter and many more. Oliver had told everyone what he'd seen and this was their response.

I burst into tears and buried my head in my pillow. What could I do? Pretend it was all a joke and go to school normally? Go to school normally and accuse Oliver of making it up just to get friends? Or stay strong and continue? I messaged Emily and told her what had happened and she said she'd had threatening messages too because she's a friend of mine. She said she was going to ignore them, stay friends with me and hit anyone who wasn't nice to me. Wow Emily sure had come out fighting.

Took deep breath and got out of bed, sat on the edge and unfriended all my new friends before going down stairs. Mum and Daisy were sitting in the kitchen drinking tea looking at each other and talking. As soon as I walked in there was silence and they both turned to look at me, just like in the films. Mum raised a half smile and asked if I wanted a cuppa. I sat down and took a sip before mum said that there had been some nasty comments sent on her social media page, mainly from people who didn't know her or me, but there had also been plenty of messages of support and offers of help to us as a family. Sadness tinged with hope. I couldn't believe that from one chance meeting there would be such a storm building up. I told mum and Daisy about the messages I'd had and the cruel words used but that I wasn't going to stop now. Mum nodded and took hold of my hands, Daisy did too and we all had a bonding cry together.

For the rest of the day we all turned our phones and computers off, watched telly and ate cake. Always helps when you're feeling low.

Monday 24ᵗʰ February

Back to school. Woke up and it was still dark, mind you that's not unusual in February. I looked at my phone and it was 5:30. Just three hours 'til hell started again but this time for real. I turned over and tried to sleep some more but my mind was racing wondering what was going to be said, done and by whom and whether the staff would try and help me. By 6:30 I decided I may as well get up and get dressed. I put my new clothes on and looked in the mirror, brushed my hair and put on a little bit of make-up (didn't want to go over the top on my first day).

I made myself some breakfast and Arthur sauntered up to me for a pat on the head and a tummy tickle. I smiled at him and he smiled back (actually I made that bit up). After a while mum and Daisy came in ready for work and school respectively and we all sat down to eat a bowl of sawdust and dried fruit called muesli. Eventually the time had come and I had to go to school. Mum drove us there and dropped us off at the gates. I was greeted by loud jeers from some boys at the gate that I didn't even know and wandered in. Emily ran to meet me and grabbed my hand and said not to worry as she was there for me at break and lunch. Wow some friends are great.

Walking into school through the front doors I was met by some of my teachers who congratulated me on my bravery and said that they would talk if I needed to. Wow some teachers are great (no, not really ha ha). I went to registration and sat down waiting for the other children to arrive. Mrs Jones walked in and sat down peering at me from over the top of her glasses. "Who are you?" she asked. "Nikki" I replied. "No, he's a boy and you're, well, not" she replied. I told her I was and asked if she'd been told by Mrs Coldheart about me living as a girl. The look on her face was something between shock and something hilarious. She composed herself and said that she didn't know. Great - communication breakdown just when I didn't need it. A few minutes later the classroom was flooded with other children. Most of the girls wanted to chat to me and sit next to me which was brilliant but all the boys just laughed and called me names. Oliver, still smelling of chips, stood in the corner of the room looking a little sheepish and stayed out of my way. I was expecting him to join in with the name calling as he's the one who told everyone, but I think he was feeling guilty. Suppose he's not that bad after all (apart from the smell).

Break and lunch were the worst parts of the day as everyone seemed to want to look at the freak wearing a skirt and tights but at least nobody hit me. Whenever I turned round there was a teacher nearby so I think Mrs

Jones was the only one who hadn't got the message. Don't think it'll be the same after the novelty has worn off.

Finally the day ended and we were allowed home. It was amazing the number of parents who had turned up to meet their children today, loads more than usual and they were all standing by their car, again probably to see the new freak girl/boy who was terrorising the school. Mum arrived as well and it was with relief that I got into the car and let out a long sigh of relief. Today hadn't been as bad as I'd imagined it to be, in fact it had better because there were lots of girls who all of a sudden wanted to be my friend. Wonder why? Anyway, not too worried as long as it doesn't get worse.

The Holiday Trousers' Diary

Tuesday 25th February

Walked to school on my own and was tripped up and laughed at by someone I'd never seen before. He stood there and giggled, called me a lezzer (?) then kicked me in the stomach winding me. Of course I cried but managed to stand and hobble off to school. This is what I'd been expecting. By the time I got there the pain had subsided enough that I could talk again without giving anything away. However, Emily knew something was wrong and told me to tell the teachers but I wouldn't because I was OK now and anyway I didn't know who it was just that he was bigger than me with a brain the size of a walnut, something that could have most of the year 10's in detention.

The Holiday Trousers' Diary

The rest of the day passed relatively incident free. There were a few insults as I walked round as well as a few names I've never heard before, probably made up to make them look macho but there were positives as well, not just from girls. It's the fact that there are these people who genuinely seem to be on my side that helps me get through the day.

When I got home I went straight to my room. My stomach was a bit tender and when I had a look there was a tick shaped bruise in purple and red forming. Oh the irony of it.

Friday 14th March

The Holiday Trousers' Diary

I've been back at school for three weeks now and it has been a struggle. Name calling, tripping, kicking, punching and being ignored are becoming the norm. Those others who have been positive are also being worn down by the morons and are beginning to keep their distance, even the teachers and as for Mrs Coldheart I haven't seen or spoken to her once since I came back to school as a girl. Last night I heard Daisy crying in her bedroom and knew what it was about. She's been picked on and it's affecting her too. She's not had the physical abuse but name calling and hearing untrue stories about your brother/sister take their toll. Even Emily, great friend and always on my side seems to be staying away from me a bit. I'm really struggling and long for the weekends when I can at least have two days away from the constant bombardment of hate.

Sunday 16th March

Spent the day with dad, Daisy stayed at home because she had too much homework (really?). Didn't wear make-up, tied my hair back and wore jeans to give the appearance of a boy, thankfully he didn't notice my shoes which had a two inch heal. He did think I'd grown though since the last time I'd seen him, hmmm. His flat hadn't improved, in fact had got worse. Dad never cleans and there was a thin layer of grease coating everything in the room. It's not often you wish to see clean duct tape. We went out for lunch, thankfully, and for a change went to a fried chicken outlet which was full of dads and their kids along with sweary groups of teenagers, something that was becoming a bit of a trend. We cleared the boxes off the table and swept the crumbs onto the floor before dad went to order. When he returned we ate in silence for a few moments savouring the taste of chicken and fat before he surprised me by asking how I was getting on at school with the changes I'd made. I nearly fell off the chair (slipped on the grease more like) and told him everything that had happened and how Daisy was too. His face clouded over and for the first time there looked a genuine sense of concern for us. He then promised to go and see the school to talk about my safety and what else they could do to help in this situation. Think this separation from us and mum has changed him.

When we'd finished eating and cleared a path through the discarded crumbs, chips and chicken bones littering the floor and got back to the car, he told me he had two surprises for me. He opened the boot and gave me a dress. I was genuinely shocked. Not just because he'd bought it for me but that it was absolutely horrendous. It was the sort of thing you might've worn at a wedding, if you had to, but not the sort of dress you'd ever wear voluntarily anywhere else. I thanked him and told him it was lovely, which going by his smile delighted him. He then said I'd have to wait a short time for the next surprise. We got in the car and drove off only to arrive ten minutes later in a pub carpark. I looked at dad quizzically and with a smile he said "Our teams live on telly and we're going to watch it." Fabulous, stuck in the corner of a pub with a bottle of coke and a packet of crisps for two hours watching a bunch of people kicking a ball surrounded by fat men wearing undersized football shirts, drinking beer and shouting at the ref/players/each other. Think I'd rather be insulted at school.

Two hours later and the score was: Pints of lager four, bottles of coke two with a red card for an out of date packet of crisps. Dad won. We left the car and walked back to the flat. The lager had loosened dad's tongue and he chatted constantly about the game and how this year there was a real chance we may finish in the top half. Is that success? No trophies and no Europe just wealthier footballers. Great!

Mum picked me up later on and I showed her my new dress. We both laughed so much she forgot to set off at the traffic lights and was hooted at by an angry looking man in a Mini. Woops.

Monday 17th March

No school today as next appointment at psychologist's. Arrived at 11:00 and sat in waiting room, this time sitting in different chair that looked uncomfortable and was. After twenty minutes had to move as circulation had been cut off to my left leg, just as Dr Sinclair came out of his office to call me in. It must have been quite a sight as I was hopping round the room and shaking my leg furiously to try and get rid of the pins and needles. He just stood there open mouthed wondering if this was a new type of dance until I explained and he just told me to come in when I was ready.

We chatted for an hour and he seemed pleased with what I'd done and how brave I'd been over the last few weeks and explained that the reactions from the other children was to be expected but that I should continue as eventually they'd give up. I was heartened by this but just wished it would stop now. Mum seemed happier too and told him that my dad seemed to be coming round to the situation and was making an effort even though his sense of style was dreadful.

Mum dropped me at home and then went off to work. I decided to do my school work and get up to date. Starting to feel much more positive. Painted my nails and watched Judge Rinder, school work could wait until later.

Friday 28th March

Last day of school before Easter. During the afternoon we had a whole school assembly where we celebrated success from each year group. I wasn't expecting anything as I hadn't done anything well or made a significant contribution to school life, so I was surprised when my name was read out for a special prize. Well meaning, but did they have to draw even more attention to what was happening? I walked out to a mixture of applause and shouts of "puffter" to the front where I was presented with a badly photocopied certificate which said "well done for being brilliant" on it. That'll certainly go in the scrap book, if I had one. Walking back one of the older children stuck their leg out and tripped me up. There was a massive cheer and laughter rang round the hall. Emily helped me up and slyly kicked the boy who'd tripped me before walking back to our places. I was really thankful she was there and for kicking the boy.

Mrs Coldheart was then presented with a small gift from the staff and a cake made into the shape of a pencil case. None of the children clapped but the staff did mainly to be polite. Nobody, it seems, liked her. I wonder if Mr Coldheart does?

By the end of the day I was more than ready to leave. I walked out the school gates clutching my certificate and looked at it again. Someone had altered it and it now said "well done for being the biggest gay puff in school." Gay puff? Isn't that like a double negative and actually means I'm straight? Anyway I tore it up and stuffed it in the nearest bin. I didn't want the extra attention or a certificate but at least it had been some recognition from the staff that what I was doing merited something. My eyes started to leak a bit until Daisy caught up with me and linked arms and we walked home together. We didn't speak about assembly. There wasn't really anything to say.

Saturday 29th March

The Holiday Trousers' Diary

First day of the Easter holidays and a time to relax and escape the turmoil of school. I was downstairs when the postman pushed through a handful of letters through the box. Arthur as usual went loopy barking at the door and trying to frighten the poor bloke doing his job. I grabbed the letters and had a look. Three looked identical and appeared to be birthday cards. There was one to mum and dad, one to Daisy and one to me. I don't often get post and was super excited to open it. I carefully pulled it open and looked at the card. It was an invitation to my Auntie Sarah's wedding in France and she wanted me to be the Page Boy. Now mum and Auntie Sarah don't often speak and she obviously hadn't told her the news of who I was now, which disappointed me a bit, especially as I didn't want to do that job. Daisy came down soon afterwards and opened hers. She was lucky and had been given the job of bridesmaid and squealed in delight. Now that's the job I wanted. When mum opened hers it invited her and dad. Again she'd not told her about dad. What were we to do?

I asked her if we were going because I wasn't sure we could afford it but mum said that Auntie Sarah's new husband was absolutely minted and that he'd agreed to pay for all our costs and pay for the outfits. But what about me being Page Boy? What about dad? This perplexed mum a little and she said she needed time to think about it, but she didn't think either would be a problem.

I was quite excited by this and Daisy and I went off to start planning the trip and what colour we'd like to wear for the wedding, like we had any choice and when would we be able to get a fitting?

Later on that evening I heard mum on the phone and she was talking to dad. I'm not sure what they were talking about but managed to hear the words "love, respect and understanding." These are words that could relate to many things. Dad makes me cross that he doesn't seem to care and doesn't try and understand but I'd still like to see him home as mum hasn't spoken about dad leaving once and has been very depressed since he went. Also that flat he lives in is awful and the other people in the house seem very odd.

Sunday 30th March

Mum phoned Aunt Sarah today. It's the first time they've spoken in ages. Mum had her phone on loud speaker so I heard the whole conversation even though she thought I was still asleep.

Mum: Hi sis how're you doing. Thanks for the invites they arrived yesterday they're beautiful and we'd love to come.

Auntie Sarah: oh fantastic, Jacques is dying to meet you all. I've told him all about you.

Mum: Ahem I'm not sure you have.

Auntie: Why? What do you mean? What's happened?

Mum: Well Des and I are on a break from each other but think we'll be back together by the time of the wedding and the other thing is, well, delicate. Are you sitting down?

Auntie: Yes. You're worrying me now.

Mum: Well, it's like this. Nikki isn't quite who you think he is.

Auntie: I don't understand.

Mum: Nikki is now a girl.

Auntie: What happened? Did you get confused with the umbilical cord when he was born? Liz it's taken a long time to notice.

Mum: No, he's grown up a bit and realized that he doesn't fit in or think like a boy and he's much more comfortable as a girl.

Auntie: OMG I bet you were mortified!

Mum: No. To tell truth think we've always known there was something different about him.

Auntie: Wow. I don't quite know what to say. Err, so does he want to be Page Boy?

Mum: No of course he doesn't, but he'd jump at the chance of being bridesmaid if that's OK with you?

Auntie: I see. Actually when you look back I suppose he's always been a bit different. Yes of course he can be bridesmaid. Wow it's all been happening at your place. Does Daisy want to be Page Boy or is she still happy as a girl?

Mum: No she's fine and can't wait to be bridesmaid.

The Holiday Trousers' Diary

Auntie: I take it that that's why you and Des are separated! He never was one for anything different. I remember him questioning why I'd want to live somewhere where they eat frog's legs.

Mum: Yea, you're right, but I've been speaking to him quite a lot recently and think he's realised what hurt he's caused especially to Nikki. We're probably going to give it another go but got to speak to the kids first to make sure they're happy with it. They're my priority.

Auntie: Well you've got to do what's right for you all but those kids come first.

Mum: I know. Anyway we'll be over second week of the summer holidays for the wedding. Thank Jacques for everything. We're dying to meet him. Oh and break the news that you've lost a nephew and gained a niece gently. Hope he understands.

Auntie: Will do. I'll send you the fabric and design for their dresses and if you can have them made up in town and bring them with you that'd be brill.

Mum: Will do. Love you. Bye.

So mum and dad are getting back together and dad's going to be more thoughtful. I hope so for all our sakes. But more importantly I'm going to be BRIDESMAID. Woohoo!

Thursday 10th April

uneventful holiday so far apart from some eggs and insults thrown at the house at midnight last night. When will they give up? Dad still not back. Maybe that's my birthday present!

Today I become a teenager.

Arthur bounded into the room at six and jumped onto the bed licking me and then wanting to go out. Thanks Arthur, remind me to do the same to you on your birthday! Maybe not.

By 8:00 I could hear movement downstairs and guessed that mum and Daisy were up. I walked down and in feigned surprise walked into the kitchen. On the table there was a massive choice of breakfast foods and a smiling mum stood at the end singing happy birthday with Daisy joining in a fraction of a second behind

which didn't have quite the effect they were going for.

Either that or it was just rubbish. Made me smile though.

I sat down and reached for a bowl of cereal, followed by

fruit and then bacon, eggs, sausage, beans, mushrooms

and hash browns finishing with toast and marmalade.

Now, because I'd started with cereal and then fruit there

were no calories in the rest (I wish). Must be careful don't

want to look too fat on my big day (actually my

Auntie's). When we'd finished eating it was card and

present time. Mum had given me money to spend in

town and Daisy had bought me the most lovely pink

pencil skirt with contrasting black blouse. Gorgeous.

Dad had dropped off a card with the message that he'd

come round tonight. I half expected a ticket to the football to drop out the card but was really pleased when there was just the message he'd written. I shall have to wait 'til this evening for my football themed gift.

I was just trying on my present from Daisy when Emily came round. She gave me the usual big hug and squealed with delight at what I was wearing giving it the Emily tick of approval, before handing me a beautifully wrapped box. I opened it not sure what would be inside and was ecstatic to find it was the newest eye shadow palette from one of the places inside the shopping centre. It couldn't have been a better day, even Daisy was excited and suggested we test them together. Nice try sis.

Emily left a little while later leaving me, mum and Daisy a little unsure what to do. We eventually decided on lunch in town rather than a trip out tonight because dad was coming round, but we'd all had so much to eat at breakfast we could hardly eat anything and so finished with soup and a roll. Following lunch we had a look round the shops and I spent some of my birthday money on a dress and a handbag but when we came out the shop we were greeted by a group of boys from school who started shouting and jeering at me and even insulting mum. I've never seen her react like that and she grabbed one of the boys and told him that if he didn't stop insulting her child she'd make sure he never spoke in a voice lower than a treble for the rest of his life. Get in mum. Woohoo.

Dad came round later and handed me a present. It was a lovely silver bracelet with a silver heart attached to it. We are definitely making progress, however, I think mum may have had a hand in this (ha ha see what I did there).

He and mum then announced that if it was ok with me and Daisy he was going to move back in. I was really pleased and told him but I also plucked up the courage to tell him that he had to understand that I really didn't like football and certainly didn't want to go and watch any games whatsoever. He grinned and said it was a deal.

What a great birthday, just hope he sticks to his word.

Monday 14th April

Back to school. Back to fear. Back to being bullied. Back to being hit. Back to misery. Back to hatred. Back to darkness.

The Holiday Trousers' Diary

I wandered up to the school gate and stopped, looking round in the hope of seeing Emily. Instead I saw Oliver and was attacked by the aroma of chips as well as a great glob of spit from him that hit my blazer on the lapel. For someone who doesn't have any friends and is bullied too, I'm always surprised that he picks on someone else. Perhaps it's because it gives him the sense of power over at least one person in the vein hope that he will be able to join the other numpties in the school. He grinned and called me a "woofter" before walking away and taking his chip smell with him. I wiped the spit off but it left a mark that seemed to set the scene for the day.

I couldn't see Emily so walked in. Mr McEwan was standing in the entrance and, in a very loud voice wished me good morning and had I had a good break.

He's the only one in school who sees the person and not

the boy wearing skirt and blouse. I told him I had and

stood chatting to him for a few minutes as this was the

only way to guarantee a break in hostilities from the

other children. Eventually the bell rang and I had to go

to lessons. French first with Madame Oriot. I spotted

Emily sitting in the corner and sat beside her. She

glanced quickly at me and managed a half smile before

saying "Bonjour." I half smiled back and wondered why

she seemed distracted. I told her my dad had come back

and that he seemed to want to do the right thing but

more importantly my mum was happy about it. Wrong

thing to say. Emily burst into tears and said her dad

had left the previous night in a foul mood and had

shouted at her and her mum. She didn't say what about. I grabbed her hand and told her not to worry as I'm sure everything would be ok even though I didn't fully believe it myself. Strangely I felt quite pleased as at last I felt I could give back something to my best friend who had supported me through the last couple of years.

By the end of the day Emily was almost her usual self but, as I knew too well, that when normality stopped and you returned to the problem that's where sadness, desperation, depression and anxiety started. I hope she's OK but know she needs to be with her mum at the moment.

Mum knew about Emily's dad but didn't give anything away so wasn't any wiser by the time dad got home from work. He was holding a bunch of flowers in the hope that he could score a few mum points and when he gave them to her she smiled, so I assume he managed to win some. He gave me and Daisy a kiss and then mentioned that his team had signed a player on loan. As soon as he said it he remembered that I wasn't interested so he apologised and said he probably wouldn't be any good anyway, as if that made any difference to me.

Thursday 17th April

Emily seems to be coming to terms with her dad leaving and is in better spirits but isn't talking about it, so maybe not.

The Holiday Trousers' Diary

Not much happened at school today apart from Joseph throwing a small piece of doweling at me in woodwork which missed and went straight into the teacher's cup of tea which made us all snigger, even me, especially when he took a drink and didn't seem the slightest bit surprised to find it there.

Getting home was different. As soon as I walked in the front door mum sat me down and said she'd had a phone call from the local newspaper, the Gazette. A reporter had heard about me (I thought everyone in the town knew already) and thought it would make an interesting piece for the paper. Mum didn't want any more publicity and neither did I to be honest. She'd said no, but thought I ought to know so I didn't think I was being kept in the dark. I asked if he'd questioned her but apparently he'd been very nice and hadn't, but she thought he might try again. I finished the day feeling very insecure and started to worry that he might try and talk to me without mum's permission, but on the other hand if he'd been nice he probably wouldn't.

Monday 21st April

I hate Mondays. It's not just the fact that there are five days of lessons it's the relentless comments and jibes that come my way from the other kids as well as the physical violence that leaves me bruised and battered by the end of the week. Today though there was a bit of excitement as someone had seen a woman taking photos from the inside of a car as we were all arriving for school this morning. I didn't believe it but thought it a bit odd.

Who'd want to do that? Surely there was a law against it

but perhaps there was an innocent reason.

Tuesday 22nd April

Usual day with people staring at me and whispering

behind raised hands. Why do people do this as it's more

obvious they're speaking and it's probably not

complimentary? No matter, more interested in making

sure Emily was ok. She seemed really down. Her dad

had been home and had taken more of his clothes. Her

mum spent the evening crying and by the looks of

Emily she had too. I assured her that this doesn't mean

he's not coming back but maybe he needs time to sort his

head out and realise what his priorities are. Emily agreed but not with much conviction and she still hasn't told me the reason he's gone. I'm not going to push her on this as I'm sure she'll tell me eventually, or mum will.

When I got home I told mum about Emily's dad which didn't seem to surprise her. She then said that she'd invited Emily and her mum over for tea on Friday as a little gesture of help and promised wine and a listening ear. Very good of mum but think she just wants to hear all the details so she can feel just that little bit superior, bit like Oliver with me I suppose.

Friday 25th April

The Holiday Trousers' Diary

Fridays are always the best day of the week at school. Nothing to do with the lessons it's just the fact that we've got two days off to look forward too. Me more than most I expect. Emily had a smile on her face and said she was excited about coming for tea and that when our mums were chatting we could have a girly evening with Daisy. What a great idea and this helped the day pass even quicker.

By the time I got home I'd made plans after chatting to Daisy about it at lunch time. When we walked in we were greeted by mum with a face like thunder holding a copy of the Gazette. She handed it over to me and gave me a hug before I had chance to read it. When she eventually let go I looked. There was a picture of me on the front cover with the headline "Trans Bully Boy Nikki Disrupts

School." Underneath (continued pages 2 and 3) there was this story about how I caused disruption to the school and picked on others for not sharing my desire to wear what I want. Further, there were stories of how the teachers knew I was a trouble causer and how I was bullying others when they didn't see eye to eye with my views. I had never read anything so utterly rubbish and knew it had been based on the testimonies of those that didn't like me, which didn't narrow it down much to who was responsible. I was also blamed for the recent poor Ofsted rating.

I cried. Mum cried. Daisy cried. How could anyone be so cruel?

Emily and her mum didn't come for tea.

I cried again.

I hate Fridays.

Monday 28th April

Didn't go to school today. Couldn't face it. In fact none of us have been out all weekend, apart from dad to the football, in fact we unplugged the phone and disconnected the internet to stop the torrent of abuse we were getting from everyone in the area. Mum seems to have aged but is adamant that I should carry on and be the person I really am.

Eventually she phoned the paper but in true diplomatic style there was no-one available to take our questions. School were slightly more helpful and promised to phone us back, but didn't. Is it really so hard for people to know the truth or does that get in the way of a sensational story? I bet the "nice" journalist hasn't got a clue how this has affected me and my family. I really thought it couldn't get any worse.

Tuesday 29th April

Plucked up the courage to go to school even though my heart wasn't in it. Was tripped once, kicked twice and spat on twice before I'd even reached the front door. Felt like turning back and running home but didn't. Once inside Mr McEwan greeted me with a smile and a loud

"how are you?" before asking, in a quieter voice if I

wanted a little chat. Once in the safety of a classroom he

told me he'd read the article and knew what a load of

rubbish it was (he didn't say rubbish ha ha). Said he'd

spoken to the head and explained that she should put out

a newsletter stating that at no time had the school

contributed to the article and that as far as we were

concerned all the allegations were completely unfounded.

This cheered me up and I asked if it had been sent out.

Apparently not and wouldn't until the head had

questioned all those who had spoken to the journalist. Of

course nobody was admitting to this so it may never

happen. Mr McEwan assured me that he was doing

everything in his power to help. At this point the bell

rang and the classroom started to fill up. Emily came in looking tired and gave me a hug. At least two people were being nice to me.

By home time I'd been called all the names under the sun. Funny how the teachers at school have selective deafness. I walked home with my head down watching the pavement. It had been a horrendous last few days and knew that if I was ever going to stand in dog poo, today was probably the day. I didn't and my shoes were clean by the time I walked through the door which was opened by mum who tried to be invisible by hiding behind the door and opening it just enough for me to squeeze through.

Once inside mum told me that she'd had a call from a national newspaper who wanted to follow up the article from the Gazette as they felt it was a human interest story. She'd agreed and they were coming round in half an hour with a photographer as well. My heart leapt and I ran upstairs to make myself more presentable.

When they arrived I looked human again and smiled when they took the photo. They spent the next hour chatting to mum about the last couple of years, ignored me and then just left. Felt deflated again. My chance to put my side of the story out there and no one wanted to know again.

Saturday 3rd May

Newspaper ran its article. Another piece of gallant British journalism missing the truth and highlighting the part of the story that they seemed most interested in, mum and dad parting for a while. They did put my picture in and I looked great but their caption suggested that I didn't care about mum, dad or school and that overall I was happy to be the centre of attention. Not sure, again, if it can get any worse.

Just as I was beginning to feel that there was no hope mum reminded me that we were going for a dress fitting for my auntie's wedding. A smile, a genuine smile, spread across my face as well as Daisy's. A chance to forget, even for a few hours, the horrors of the last few days. We parked up in the multi-storey and weaved our way between the Saturday shoppers, ignoring a few who recognised us from the newspapers and made our way to the wedding dress shop. Once inside we gave our names but the assistant remembered us and we took a seat while she fetched the dresses. Daisy and I went to the changing rooms and tried our dresses on. Mine fitted beautifully and when I walked out mum's face lit up and the assistant clapped her hands and shrieked in delight. I felt wonderful, the past few days melted behind me. Wow there is a future after all. Daisy looked stunning too and when we stood side by side mum insisted on taking a picture and instantly uploaded it to social media not caring what the world thought as she had the two most gorgeous daughters in the world.

When we left we decided to be brave and went out for lunch. We went to one of those burger type places and had a lovely meal made even better when the manager came over and told us it was on the house. He'd had a run in with the journalist of the local paper before and knew the article was probably made up. He wished us luck and said we could drop in anytime and there'd always be a smile waiting for us. Think mum would've preferred more free food though. It just shows that not everyone is horrible.

By the time we got home we were all tired but as we opened the door the phone was ringing. Mum picked it up with some trepidation. It was Emily's mum and she'd rung to apologise about the other evening explaining that things had got on top of her and the article hadn't helped even though she knew it was rubbish. Mum started crying again, but this time in a good way and arranged for them to come round the following Friday.

The Holiday Trousers' Diary

One of the worst weeks of my life had finished really positively. Happy(ish) again.

Monday 5th May

School again. Mum sent me on my own only to discover nobody there. I hoped that everyone had been packed off to Mars on a Government funded experiment to see if idiots could survive on their own in space, but no, it was May Day Bank Holiday. Now I felt the idiot for not remembering. Walked back home to find mum and dad both out. Ha ha they'd both forgotten too. Sat down and watched TV for a while. Jeremy Kyle was shouting at people telling them to get a grip even on a bank holiday. Doesn't he ever get a day off, or more to the point don't the viewing public? Dad arrived home soon after whistling a happy tune obviously delighted about forgetting the one day break and was soon followed by mum who was humming a happy tune to herself. They made a coffee and asked Daisy and I if we fancied a ride out somewhere for the day.

An hour later we set off not knowing where we were going and not caring either it was just much better than the day we'd expected. Twenty minutes later we arrived at a Scandinavian furniture shop on the outskirts of town. Not the trip I'd expected but maybe we'd get something for our rooms. After driving round for what seemed like an eternity we found a parking spot and headed towards the entrance fighting against the crowd of hot-dog eating shoppers leaving with their luminous cushions and flat pack bedside tables. Once inside we followed the route round the store occasionally stopping to test out a chair/mattress/kitchen stool until we caught sight of Emily's dad. He was discussing the merits of buying something with a tall long legged woman who was wearing a rather nice pair of leather trousers and plain white t-shirt. At first I thought it was a strange outfit to wear to work until I realised that this was the reason he'd left Emily and her mum. I tried pointing them out to mum but she'd already seen them and was beginning to turn a rather nice shade of red and her fists had become clenched like she was about to have a fight. Dad was completely oblivious to this and was still grinning at a joke he'd made about one of the Scandinavian names on one of the products and didn't have time to stop mum marching across the shop floor and confronting the two of them in a very unladylike and loud manner. I should have done or said something to help but mum seemed in control and within a few seconds had quite a large crowd of people surrounding her where most of the women were nodding their heads in agreement and the men were tutting or not saying anything at all. Eventually when mum had finished, Emily's dad and his girl-friend walked away to a few cheers, a couple of hand claps and great many telling mum how she'd been right and that they agreed with what she'd said. Wow, this afternoon suddenly got better, but should I tell Emily or not?

We finished our walk round and by the end mum had toned down her enraged look to one that said "I'm a bit cross." Dad hadn't said a word apart from "well that told him." Think he was too frightened of mum by this point and decided that if he said anything it would probably be wrong. There were no purchases today apart from dad bought some meatballs and jam and also four hotdogs because they were what everyone else did, before pushing through the line of people waiting to get the two screws they were short of in their furniture they'd bought yesterday, and walked back to the car. There were still families driving round looking for spaces and I'm sure a couple of them were there when we arrived. I can't imagine what the conversation inside would have been like.

Once home mum suggested we go upstairs and tidy our rooms, which was code for "I've got an important call to make and I don't want you to hear." The three of us trudged upstairs (yes, even dad) knowing that to argue was not a good idea, and went into our rooms. We all tidied very quietly with our doors slightly open so that we could hear what mum was saying and from her reaction guess how the other person (Emily's mum) had replied. After about half an hour we were allowed down again and mum put the tea on. She'd calmed down a bit more and said she'd spoken to Emily's mum and explained what had happened, which we all knew already but pretended not to, and that she was coming to terms with the fact that he was a "lying, cheating scumbag." Wow mum we weren't expecting that. I asked if I was allowed to say anything to Emily and mum said I could as Emily knew everything. Poor Emily, my best friend was having a tough time but at least I could now speak to her about it and hopefully help her.

Those leather trousers were nice though.

Tuesday 6th May

Mum's argument and red faced explosion yesterday was the talk of the school. For a change people weren't talking about me but for Emily there was embarrassment because now everyone knew why her dad had left and that he'd been embarrassed in the middle of a Scandinavian furniture store on one of their busiest days of the year. Emily was inconsolable and her face was covered in dirty black marks where her mascara had run and red eyes from rubbing them with a soggy tissue. Madame Oriot was the only person in the school who didn't seem to know and asked Emily "Ca Va?" If she was Ok in front of the class. Not a good move and probably prolonged the crying even more as she insisted she answer "en Francais." I wanted to give Emily a hug like she'd done for me so many times but knew I'd have to wait until later.

Later came, and she seemed to have calmed down, well, enough to stop crying even though there were still some cruel jibes from people who should know better. I reminded her of Friday as I couldn't wait and was pleased she responded with a half-smile which is better than none.

The Holiday Trousers' Diary

Friday 9th May

Spent this morning thinking what a great day at school it was. I was excited because Emily and her mum were coming for tea and we were going to have our long awaited girly night. That was until Emily told me that her dad was coming round for a chat with mum and that they'd be coming over after he left, if he left early enough. Disappointed wasn't the word, deflated was.

By the time we'd got to the evening I'd resigned myself to the fact that they weren't coming based on various other condemning factors during the day, for instance I couldn't use my lucky mug as it was in the dishwasher when I got home, I saw a magpie on its own on the way back and Daisy had taken a different route to me whilst chatting to a boy, all proof indeed that my luck was out today.

By 7:00pm they still weren't here and I'd settled down for an evening of soaps and dad grumbling that Friday telly was crap, when there was a knock at the door. Emily stood there looking gorgeous next to her mum who looked ok but who, maybe needed to chat to let a few things out. I beamed with delight as did dad who saw this visit as an excuse to go to the pub for the evening. Result for the two of us. Mum was relieved too as she'd spent the last twenty minutes reading the microwave instructions on the back of our tea and didn't want that time going to waste. Even Daisy was pleased, but not really sure why.

The Holiday Trousers' Diary

Me, Emily and Daisy went upstairs whilst mum and Emily's mum went into the kitchen and closed the door ready to verbally assassinate Emily's dad, empty a bottle of wine or two and discuss ways of moving forward before ~~cooking~~ microwaving a meal for us all to ~~enjoy~~ eat.

Once upstairs we all sat on my bed and got as much makeup out as we could find and started practising on ourselves as well as each other. I couldn't get the grin off my face. This is what I'd been looking forward to for the last couple of weeks, however, some of the results were great but others just made us look like scary clowns. More work needed. For the first half hour we didn't hear anything from downstairs but eventually the wine kicked in and the voices seemed to become louder and louder before the tears started flowing from both of them.

These eventually subsided and we heard the call for tea, a loud ping from the microwave and went downstairs to find a lovely meal prepared for us by supermarket own brand and warmed by mum. Well done Mr or Mrs Own Brand.

Tea finished and our mums cleared the plates before sitting down staring at me and Emily with stern looks on their faces. Mum started and said that they'd been chatting and stated that they knew how unhappy we both were at school and they both felt that it would be a good idea if we had a fresh start at a new school where nobody knew us and that as we were such good friends it would be right that we both moved to the same school rather than just one of us. Well this was a surprise and one that took a few moments to sink in. I looked at Emily at the same time she looked at me. We both smiled and hugged each other. A great idea and we wouldn't be apart. Daisy then asked "What about me?" and was told that she could stay if she wanted but if she'd prefer she could move schools as well. Queue three girls squealing and hugging at the same time. I looked over at mum and Emily's mum who were both smiling the biggest smiles I'd seen in a long time. Even Arthur was caught up in the celebrations and ran over to us wagging his tail, probably hoping he'd get a treat for joining in. What a good boy! We went upstairs and sat talking about which schools were around us and which uniform would look best before watching a film and letting the realisation of what had happened this evening sink in.

Daisy and Emily were no doubt thinking the same but none of us were complaining.

Realised it didn't guarantee I'd be happy but at least there was a chance, and I'd have my sister and best friend with me.

Monday 12th May

Didn't tell anyone at school, because there wasn't anyone to tell, but a few people noticed that I looked happier which must have annoyed them as they took the opportunity to ramp up the insults and kick a little harder. I tried not to let it affect me but couldn't help feel down. How many weeks to go?

The Holiday Trousers' Diary

Friday 16th May

Strange week. Happy then sad before happy again.

Have been to the doctors and the psychologist who have agreed that I definitely want to be a girl and have suggested that I start to take some drugs that stop puberty so that I don't start looking like a man in drag with a beard and deep voice. I know this doesn't make me a real girl but it's the next step of the journey that I know I want. Dad even thought it was the right thing for me and gave me a hug. Wonder if he's been taking something too or whether he has at last come to the realisation that this is what I want. Hooray.

Told Emily and she was really pleased for me but said her dad was completely the opposite and seemed further away than ever. Apparently this woman he's been seeing doesn't want to meet Emily yet but her dad has met her children and they're all living together. How can anyone do that to their own child? There always seems something that brings you down from the height you got to.

Emily was there for me so I must be there for Emily.

Monday 2nd June

First day of the last half term at this school. Exams loom so at least I've got something to focus on and then the summer holidays with the prize of being bridesmaid at my aunt's wedding. Our new school has been decided upon and we're off to one ten miles away which may seem a long way but at least nobody knows me or reads the local paper and can make a prejudiced judgement. The uniform is lovely. It's burgundy with a pleated knee length skirt, white blouse, blue and burgundy tie and blazer. Mum has told the head teacher all about me and he's fine with it. In fact he's more than fine as he sees it as a learning opportunity for his children and staff and believes that all schools should do more to embrace diversity as a way of becoming more tolerant of the world around them. He's even guaranteed my happiness and safety. Not sure he can fully do that but at least it's good to hear. Wow, what a difference from where I am now, a place that seems to embrace insults and violence as a way of coping with the modern world.

The Holiday Trousers' Diary

Emily and Daisy are happy too about the new place and seem as eager as I am to start. Daisy and Emily haven't had the same treatment from the other kids as I have, but through association they've had their fair share of trauma, though don't think they've told me about it all which is good as I'd have been even more depressed if I'd known.

Met Emily after school and walked home together. She seems a bit happier at home. Her mum seems to be accepting the situation more and has started divorce proceedings. Not a great thing to have to go through but, like me, you have to make steps for the future. Her dad has been a bit shocked by this and has seen Emily on a couple of occasions which by all accounts were a bit nervy for both of them. That woman hasn't met her yet though and it's getting to the point where Emily doesn't want to meet her either. Hope they can patch things up. Me and dad did even when I thought there was no hope.

Monday 9th June

First day of exams. English language and history today. We all sat in this large room that we'd never been in before at desks that were slightly too big for us in rows that we'd never sat in before. If they were trying to make this more difficult for us to do well they were doing a good job. Oliver sat next me and the "eau de chip" perfume he was wearing made me feel sick. A boy I didn't know sat behind me and coughed the words "poofter" every few minutes and gently kicked my chair to make me feel even more uncomfortable. I shuffled my table and chair forward which helped but this didn't stop his cough. I turned to look at Oliver but he just grinned before sticking one finger up at me, probably explaining the number of questions he was able to answer. Can't wait to change schools.

After what seemed like an eternity we were allowed to start and thankfully found that I could answer all the questions. Either I fully concentrated on the exam or the boy's cough got better but the time flew and I came out of the exam pleased with what I'd written. Everyone was talking about how they'd answered but each time I tried to join in they'd shut me out and say they weren't interested in what I'd put. When I found Emily she said she'd done her best but wasn't sure that was good enough. I'm sure it is.

History followed pretty much the same pattern, as the places we'd been given in the morning were the places we had to sit in for all the exams. Great, chips to one side and a vulgar cough behind me. Mustn't let it get to me.

Friday 13th June

Last day of exams.

Maths first which went well and was made even better when I caught Oliver out of the corner of my eye using his fingers to count. It could have been funnier if he'd used his toes as well but glad he didn't as the smell of his feet might be even worse than his usual aroma.

The Holiday Trousers' Diary

At the end of the exam there was a group sigh of relief and a dropping of pens and pencils on the desk before a synchronised turning to the person next to you and smiling, even if you didn't feel like it. Relief they were all over.

We thought that we'd be able to go home for the afternoon but had to stay and we were "treated" to an afternoon of sport. I hate sport. I changed on my own and joined the pack outside on the field. Today's sport was long distance running. That's not a sport it's a torture. We had to run in groups with the winners progressing through to a final. When my group started I was in the lead and beginning to think it wasn't so bad after all. I glanced behind me and saw a boy catching up with me and expected him to pass but instead he just barged into me knocking me to the floor and trampled on my back.

As the others passed they did the same and I could hear

their laughs one by one and the teacher's voice shouting

from a distance to "Get up, don't be so soft and keep

running." Thanks for the help. When I got back, last

and bruised, all the other children just laughed at me

and pretended to wipe their eyes with imaginary tissues.

I hate them.

Didn't bother telling mum and dad as they'd go to the

school, complain, it'd be investigated and I'd be accused

of lying because there would be so many others

contradicting my story. Bed, bruised and battered.

Thursday 17th July

Very excited. Tomorrow is the last day of school and I'm leaving. Can't wait. Lessons are a bit of a joke as the teachers can't be bothered and even if they could the children can't and they wouldn't be allowed to teach effectively. Me and Emily have spent as much time together as we can to avoid the idiots and braindead who are in our year and have pretty much succeeded. We did pretty well in our exams and laughed at how badly some of the others did. Apparently, Oliver only spelt one word correctly in his English exam and it wasn't chips but was fries. Don't actually know if that's true but it made us laugh.

When we left today we knew we weren't coming back. Our mums had told us we were not going in for the last day just in case the others found out and decided to have one last punch, kick or insult at our expense. As I walked through the gate for the last time I looked back and all I could see were angry faces, punches and kicks aimed at me and insults flying everywhere. These last two years have been the worst of my life and at last were ending. I turned away from the school and in front of me I could see the sunshine beginning to rise above the horizon and feel happiness filling my soul. I just hope that it's not false and that there is something to look forward to. Not sure how Emily was feeling but I'm pretty sure it was the same sort of thing. Daisy caught up with us and put her arms around both our shoulders. She grinned at us both in turn and we knew that this nightmare was over.

Sunday 27th July

Set off for France today. Over the past week I've felt myself become more positive and am so looking forward to our trip. Me and Daisy picked up our dresses for the wedding and we look gorgeous in them. Dad says you can't tell I'm a boy. Thanks dad I know you mean well but sometimes you say things without thinking. We're staying in a small gite 3 miles from the wedding in a large chateau. There are going to be 250 guests so we've got to look perfect. Dad has bought a new suit. He chose it himself but only after mum told him that it was a good choice. Mum has also bought some new clothes and has got a lovely flowery dress in pink and purple with purple high heeled shoes. She looks great but now towers over dad. We're even taking Arthur with us and he's got a new collar with a bow tie attached to the front and looks very smart, just hope he doesn't start trying to sniff all the guests or bark through the hymns. Auntie insisted we bring Arthur to the wedding saying he's part of the family and he shouldn't be left out. Fingers crossed she doesn't regret this invitation.

Monday 28th July

Arrived at the accommodation after a long journey. Mum and dad emptied the car whilst me and Daisy put on our swimsuits and tested the pool. It's very good but colder than I thought it would be. Arthur tried it too but didn't wear a swimsuit. He swam around for about 20 minutes going round in circles with his head sticking out the water. He got out just as mum came out to sit down and shook himself all over her. Well at least that cooled mum down a bit. Dad laughed. Wrong move dad. After driving for hours he'd just won the "cooking for the family tonight" prize after he'd got back from the supermarket. Congratulations!

Dad cooked us a lovely meal and we all played cards outside on the terrace and watched the sun go down. It's not often we all do something together like this and it was a really good night. I wish we could just bottle this feeling up and keep it for other times. When it was time for bed Arthur slept in our room as a treat but kept most of us up all night as he kept barking at the different noises outside. Still, it all adds to the holiday memories.

The Holiday Trousers' Diary

Tuesday 29th July

We all went over to auntie's house. She welcomed us all with the biggest smile I've seen from her and a hug that wouldn't have looked out of place in a wrestling match. I genuinely thought I was never going to breathe again. She stood back and took a long look at us and said "I thought you were bringing my nephew with you not this gorgeous new niece I can see before me?" I know she's my auntie but she couldn't have made me feel any better and more accepted than she just had. After a quick coffee we then travelled on to see the venue for the wedding. Wow it suddenly hit home how big it was and how many people were going to be there filling it up. Suddenly I had butterflies in my stomach and by the look of Daisy she had too. Auntie was great and put our minds at rest when she said that although people would be looking at us they'd probably be watching her more. Good point. There was a run through of events and timings and we were given our instructions where to stand, sit etc. before being taken outside to check where the photos were being taken. Dad started early and took a few snaps which he said would be good to compare once we saw the official pictures. Then it was back to auntie's for lunch and a relax on the veranda, looking out over the hills and surrounding countryside. Arthur had been very excited earlier on but now just yawned and lay down with his head on the floor and his eyes shut, occasionally opening one of them to check out a buzzing insect. Mum was in her element and chatted away to her sister without drawing breath. It seemed every subject that could be covered was discussed and many more in between. Eventually though we made our way back to the gite and had a long awaited dip in the pool. Dad cooked again and by the look on his face when we went in to eat he'd been helped by a couple of bottles of wine. Another good meal but the cards ended up just the three of us as dad snored through the evening before waking up and stating that he probably needed to go to bed as the journey yesterday was catching up on him. Mum scowled.

Saturday 2nd August

Day of the wedding. We all got up early to give us time to get ready without rushing. Doesn't happen really. Me and Daisy were ready first. We felt wonderful in our bridesmaid's dresses and waited for the lady to arrive who was going to do our makeup for us. She arrived and made us look fantastic before starting on mum who also looked stunning. Dad was last to be ready and we only just managed to set off in time for the chateau and to meet up with auntie. We needn't have worried as she arrived fashionably late. We followed her in, our faces beaming. Inside, what seemed like thousands of people turned to look at us as we walked up the aisle to take our places next to the groom, Jacques, who looked very handsome and smiled when he saw us all. Once we'd delivered her to the front we took our places and joined with the other guests listening to the service.

The Holiday Trousers' Diary

When we'd got the invites I was surprised Arthur had been invited, even more surprised he'd gone to the service and was absolutely mortified when he joined in with the hymns howling away from somewhere at the back. He'd never shown any interest in Songs of Praise before so to hear him try and sing now was a shock. I turned round to see if anyone had noticed and most of the congregation were looking round to see where this strange noise had come from. How embarrassing.

Eventually Jacques kissed the bride and we made our way outside to a sea of flashing cameras and smiles that must have kept quite a number of dentists in luxury over the previous few years. I could see mum, but dad and Arthur were absent so I looked around only to see him walking out the chateau tying up a poo bag that looked rather full. I found out later that the excitement had got too much for Arthur after his help with the singing and dad had had to find some cleaning materials and a scrubbing brush before being allowed out.

We moved on to the reception where we were treated to a feast of French cuisine and a set of speeches in both French and English, followed by a disco. Mum and dad by this time were well in the swing of things and enjoying the free drinks a little too much. Dad's tie was half way down his chest and he'd caused much uproar in the venue when he did a solo dance to "The Birdie Song" which once seen cannot be unseen, a sentiment felt by all I should think. Mum wasn't much better and had insisted on singing karaoke style to Celine Dion's

Titanic anthem which cleared the dance floor and put back the celebrations a good 20 minutes. Mum has a wonderful voice, if you're deaf. It wasn't long after these two events that a taxi arrived to take us back to the gite. Both mum and dad swear they don't remember ordering it but we went back anyway.

Once back they went straight to bed and within minutes could hear snoring. I chatted to Daisy for a while and we both agreed that it had been a fantastic day apart from dad dancing and mum singing. I didn't want to take my dress off and clean my makeup off as I wanted to stay like this forever. But before doing so I managed to smile at myself in the mirror knowing that nobody had realised I wasn't a real girl. I will be one day.

The Holiday Trousers' Diary

Tuesday 26th August

We've been back home for a couple of weeks now and I think mum and dad's apologies have been accepted for their behaviour at the wedding. I told Emily all about it when we got back which made her laugh but she's had a miserable summer. Her mum and dad have been arguing about Emily and where she should be spending her time. Her dad's new girlfriend has now met her which is good but still think there's a lot of work still to be done between the two of them. It's funny how parents argue like this and forget to ask the most important person what their opinion is. I just hope they do something soon because I'm worried about my friend.

We start our new school in a week and this is keeping us both excited and nervous in equal measures. Our uniforms are ready and we already have our lifts to school written down in the form of a timetable drawn up by our mum's. We're going to make the most of our last few days before hard work begins, hopefully in safety this time.

Wednesday 3rd September

First day of school and starting on a Wednesday means it's a short week that will ease us into the start of our new lives. I was up really early and dressed ready to go almost an hour before we were due to set off. Daisy was the same and a text from Emily confirmed that all three of us were raring to go. That hour we had to wait for our lift seemed like one of the longest in history. Breakfast telly smiled at us from the corner of the room but its mix of news and celebrity failed to make time move quicker.

At last Emily and her mum arrived and we were wished good luck from our parents before jumping in the car. Traffic held us up a bit but we arrived in time and walked through the gates. What a difference. Nobody swore at me or kicked or punched me. Other children were smiling and chatting to each other. Teachers in the entrance talked with the children and asked them about their summer holidays. When we walked in we were greeted by the head and deputy who shook our hands and said how delighted they were that we had started and if there were any problems we had to see them straight away. They showed us to our classrooms, Daisy first and then me and Emily in the same one before calling over a few other children who had been assigned

to help us find our way round and generally help us

settle in. They were all so nice and chatted excitedly

wanting to know all about us, where we lived and tell us

about all the different teachers and staff at the school.

One of the girls, Afshar, took me to one side and told me

that everyone in the school knew about me. For a second

my heart dropped as I thought this was the start of a new

nightmare, but instead she smiled and said all the

children and staff were on my side and they all thought

how brave I was. For some reason I started crying and

Emily rushed to my side but she could see I wasn't upset,

it was just relief that I was going to be accepted for being

me and not judged by ignorance.

When the bell rang we all took a seat and waited in silence for our teacher, Mrs Ayling, to take the register. She made a special point of welcoming me and Emily to both the class and school and told us her door was always open if we needed to talk. From there we made our way to the hall for a special "new year" assembly. Everyone sat in silence and we listened to the head talk to us about the coming months and confirming the expectations of the school. I glanced at Emily and we both read each other's minds, knowing that this was where we would be happy and the future wasn't going to be quite as tough. Yes we've both got hurdles to clear, but the future really does start here.

Wednesday 31st December

The Holiday Trousers' Diary

I've just looked at my diary and there's nothing written for the last few months, well nothing of real note. Life has changed. Yes there's still the odd comment but life is now happy for all of us. Emily has settled into a routine where she goes to her dad's for part of the week and stays with her mum the rest of the time. Me and Daisy couldn't be happier. We've made new friends and we're both doing really well in all our subjects.

As for home life, well mum and dad are happier than I've seen them for a long time. It's probably due to the fact that dad has accepted me for who I am and there isn't the constant worry of me being bullied, that they've had to put up with for the last few years.

Tonight they're having a party and have invited quite a few people. I'm wearing my holiday trousers that still

AUTHOR - N E SYKES

look great and more importantly still fit. I've got Emily and Afshar coming over to join in the celebrations too. Not sure what they've let themselves in for though as dad's started on the wine already and is humming the "Birdie Song" and mum has insisted that at some time tonight there's karaoke. Arthur's staying out the way.

Life's looking good. Here's to the future.

Happy New Year? Yes, I think it might be!

Printed in Great Britain
by Amazon

86982604R00161